A MOST EXCELLENT UNDERSTANDING

WADE H. MANN

Quills & Quartos
PUBLISHING

Edited by Deborah Styne and Regina McCaughey-Silvia

Cover design by Hoja Designs

ISBN 978-1-956613-27-8 (ebook) and 978-1-956613-28-5 (paperback)

This story is dedicated to the love of my life, my wife Amalia, and to my daughters Selena and Clara. Together, we built a family, a successful business and the very best time of our lives.

I met my wife in Madrid the middle of a 12,000-mile bike trip. She very bravely joined me for the last five, and we have been in love for the better part of two decades. Everything good in my life is centered around my wife and daughters, and I consider myself a very lucky man.

CHAPTER ONE

Tour of the Park

"What he told me was merely this: that he congratulated himself on having lately saved a friend from the inconveniences of a most imprudent marriage, but without mentioning names or any other particulars, and I only suspected it to be Bingley from believing him the kind of young man to get into a scrape of that sort, and from knowing them to have been together the whole of last summer."

"Did Mr Darcy give you reasons for this interference?"

"I understood that there were some very strong objections against the lady."

— *PRIDE & PREJUDICE, CHAPTER 33*

"I SEE. DID MR DARCY SPECIFY THE CAUSE OF THE separation? Was it the lady herself or perhaps her family or situation?"

"He only told me what I have now told you," replied Colonel Richard Fitzwilliam.

Elizabeth Bennet walked on in thoughtful, confused silence for a few moments.

Who could possibly—absent some type of congenital malady—object to Jane?

Elizabeth would never claim to be the smartest woman in the world, but she was far from stupid. At the very least, she was not the silliest of her sisters, although that did not give her much reason to boast. However, she had to think about the conundrum for several minutes before a completely rational explanation occurred to her. Elizabeth was so thrilled to have the problem understood, she immediately set about using her newfound intelligence to make corrections.

Almost in a whisper, she said, "That explains everything!"

The colonel arched a brow and tipped his head in enquiry.

She sighed. "I see you are confused. Do not distress yourself on my account, sir. You have simply given me some things to think about, so my thoughts have been engaged."

"Would you care to explain your thoughts, if that is not too personal a question?"

"You might not like them, Colonel."

He shrugged. "By all means, keep your privacy if you prefer. I would gladly listen to your feelings should you wish it, but I shall not insist."

Elizabeth looked at him in mild amusement. He was an amiable, gentleman-like man—aside from his obvious propensity for gossip and complete lack of sense—but the few hours she had spent with him were sufficient. With some people such as her cousin, Mr Collins, a little time in their presence is enough. With someone like Colonel Fitzwilliam, perhaps a moderate time might be appropriate. Either way, Elizabeth had just about had her fill of his company.

She took a deep breath. "What I am thinking, while entirely just and proper and possibly of some use to you, might be considered outside the bounds of propriety."

"I have been fighting on the Continent for years, madam. I am somewhat resilient," he replied gallantly. "Fear no censure from me, Miss Bennet. If you wish to talk, I shall listen. If not, I shall leave you in peace."

Elizabeth thought for a moment. "Would you be willing to keep a confidence, Colonel? Most particularly, from your cousins?"

"It would be my honour, madam."

Elizabeth sighed in annoyance. It was one thing finally to have the missing piece that explained everything, a certain amount of relief to be had in finally knowing. It was quite another thing to be satisfied with what it entailed.

"Very well, sir. I shall enlighten you, as I shall request your assistance."

"I am at your disposal."

"I can assure you that your cousin omitted relevant details, but your surmise was correct. It was the lady's family that Mr Darcy found unsuitable enough to peel Mr Bingley away while abandoning the county. The lady herself is the sweetest, kindest, gentlest, most loving, and most thoughtful creature ever to walk the face of the earth. Unlike the Bingleys, she is gently born, so she would raise his social status. Unlike Mr Bingley's sisters, the lady is fully trained and skilled in the management of an estate. She is kind and polite to everyone from prince to pauper. It does not hurt her cause that she is the most beautiful woman I ever met."

She saw she had the colonel's undivided attention. "Aside from a modest dowry, even a black-hearted man like your cousin would be hard-pressed to find a single fault with my eldest sister," she concluded.

The colonel gasped, much as she expected. Elizabeth might have enjoyed the ridiculousness of the scene if she were not in the middle of it.

With a sigh, she delivered the final blow. "You see, Mr Darcy separated his friend from my sister Jane because of her family. More specifically, he separated them because of me."

"No, this is impossible! I cannot believe it. On what basis could you state such a conclusion?"

Elizabeth studied him carefully. "I fear this entire incident has pointed out a flaw in my discernment. I am not as clever or observant as I thought. I prided myself on my abilities. I always thought myself an excellent judge of character. I made it a major occupation to study people and thought perhaps I had some modest skill."

"I have no reason to doubt that."

"Yet, I now find that I so thoroughly misjudged your cousin as to be beyond all hope of redemption. Now that I know the full story, I find myself mortified that I did not see it before. All the signs were there, as obvious as a fire in your bed, yet I was caught completely unaware. Your tale explains everything, but I should have worked it out myself some time ago. I feel so very stupid!"

The colonel stared at her, brows furrowed, and finally asked in confusion, "You see what, Miss Bennet? If you are seeking to enlighten me, you are not quite there yet, or frankly, even close."

Elizabeth wondered how much to tell the man, particularly since Mr Darcy would no doubt learn of it eventually. Since she had no chance of seeing either gentleman after she left Kent, she thought it to be of no particular importance either way. If it made the *gentleman* uncomfortable to be caught out, so much the better.

"You see, Colonel, Mr Darcy and I have always had a disinclination for each other. Neither of us liked the other very much from the first moments of our acquaintance—nay, before we were even introduced. I always thought it was a mild mutual antipathy. Now I see his disapprobation was far worse than I imagined. I have no idea why, but I can plainly see he despises me. It must have been greatly vexing for him to have to tolerate my company this fortnight. I am surprised he remained, to tell the truth."

"Pardon me, but you make no sense! What evidence have you? I cannot believe Darcy dislikes you as you suppose."

Elizabeth could see the colonel wished to defend his cousin. Any man would, so she would not hold it against him. She would, however, take his natural bias towards his own family into account.

"For six weeks last autumn, Mr Darcy was in Hertford-shire at his friend's leased estate, which is adjacent to my father's. We met at an assembly where he took an almost instant dislike of me. In fact, his disdain caused him to insult me loudly and publicly before we exchanged a single word. After that, we were frequently in company and spent the entire time going out of our way to cause mutual vexation. I always believed he only had a mild dislike, matching my own senti-ments. He was constantly staring at me in disapproval or arguing with almost every word that escaped my mouth. He even accused me of professing opinions that in fact were not my own, as though I had to go out of my way to argue with him. Now I can see it was something much stronger than I imagined."

The colonel looked at her in disbelief. "You say he insulted you?"

"At a public assembly, he said I was 'barely tolerable and not handsome enough to tempt him' to dance. He even claimed I was being 'slighted by other men' because I sat out a dance and said he would not 'lend me consequence' in my own neighbourhood! All this occurred when we had not even been introduced."

She looked at her companion. Clearly aghast, his mouth hung open.

Sighing in resignation, she continued. "After that, I assumed he mildly disliked me. He even danced with me once, which I presume was a bet gone wrong. Apparently, he found the experience so unpleasant that his entire party, including his friend who had been showing strong attention to my sister for six weeks, decamped at first light the next day and were never heard from again except for one rather unpleasant letter from Miss Bingley."

Colonel Fitzwilliam appeared deep in thought as they walked towards the parsonage. "Is this the entire basis of your assertion, Miss Bennet?"

"Is that insufficient? To strip his friend from my sister and cause him to abandon an estate, less than two months into a one-year lease, seems reasonably clear to me. What was it you said? I believe the words 'strong objections to the lady' came from the so-called gentleman's own lips? He said it in what he presumed was a private conversation. Those are his words, not mine! He never spoke more than a few words to anyone in my family except me."

Darcy will have my head.

Colonel Fitzwilliam cursed himself for bringing up the topic of Darcy's goodness to his friend. He thought his cousin might be partial to Miss Bennet and imagined a rousing story of a rescue from a fortune-hunter might raise him in her esteem, but far from congratulating him on the success of the endeavour as expected, she seemed deeply angry at Darcy—apparently with cause.

The colonel did not know whether to be more offended at Miss Bennet's characterisation of his cousin as a black-hearted villain, or her insinuation that she herself was somehow to blame. Everything about their exchange had him wanting to defend both parties.

"Is there anything else, Miss Bennet?"

She looked as though she might laugh. "Allow me to ask a question you can discern with your own eyes. Have you ever witnessed a single interaction between Mr Darcy and I that showed anything beyond the barest of civilities? How much time does your cousin spend staring out of windows when not in my presence? How often does he call on people out of the barest civility required of a gentleman, yet refrains from saying more than half a dozen words for the entire visit? How often does he leave the entire burden of conversation to you?"

He had to admit the lady had a point. Darcy had been much more taciturn during this visit than usual. Although it pained him to admit it, the presence of a lady for whom he had a strong but thoroughly unreasonable aversion might explain his silence. Darcy had been hunted by the most viciously determined ladies of the *ton* for a decade and had the strong instincts necessary to survive such a hostile environment. He often remarked that his good opinion once lost, was lost forever. If Miss Bennet had lost his good opinion, it would explain everything.

Thinking further, the colonel reflected that he had no idea if Darcy ever called on the parsonage alone. He certainly made no effort to be even minimally sociable when they visited together. Miss Bennet's assertion held together with logical consistency if nothing else. Darcy was even polite to their aunt's idiot parson, and George Wickham was still breathing air instead of worms. Darcy tried—but apparently failed—always to maintain his good manners, no matter how much he disliked someone. He was even polite to Bingley's youngest sister, which required preternatural levels of self-control.

The colonel finally admitted defeat. "Although I can find no fault with your argument, the entire situation leaves me begging for another explanation. Please do not consider this forward, but I find it impossible to dislike you. I have a difficult time thinking so poorly of my cousin. It is most perplexing!"

"You are begging for an explanation over a question of a few moments' entertainment with your cousin, sir. My sister, on the other hand, is begging for the man who courted her for six weeks and abandoned her without a single word on Mr Darcy's instructions. My sister, the best person in the world, has already suffered months of my mother's harangues, and continues to suffer her own broken heart and the neighbourhood's derision for her disappointed hopes."

The colonel kicked a rock out of the path in a show of contrition and thought for some time. "I can see no fault with your logic, but Darcy cannot possibly be that stupid."

Miss Bennet laughed. "You apparently take a dim view of your cousin since your assertion logically opines that he is at least reasonably stupid."

He joined in her laughter and wondered whether Miss Bennet had any fortune to speak of. Unlike Darcy, he was not a blind fool. Of course, it was not ideal to try wooing a lady when she was furious, but he still had three days in the county to talk to her again, and it would not be at all hard to locate her later.

"In that surmise, you are entirely correct. My cousin is a man of extremes. He is either the cleverest man I know or the stupidest, depending on context."

When she nodded with an expression of confusion on her countenance, he asked, "May I assist you in some way?"

"Would you grant me a small favour?"

"Ask, and if it can be done, it will be."

"Is Mr Darcy at Rosings now?"

"No, he is out dealing with a tenant issue."

"Perfect," she said, giving him a relieved smile. "I believe your aunt likes to be of use. Might you escort me to Rosings and arrange for a short private interview with Lady Catherine, without anyone else being aware? I would like to ask a favour."

The colonel did not like the sound of that, but he had given his word, so he simply took the next turn in the path towards Rosings. He thought about trying to dissuade the lady, but nothing in her demeanour suggested she was one to be worked on with anything short of a block and tackle. Certainly, anyone who would willingly ask his aunt for help or advice was not to be trifled with.

They had walked in silence for a few minutes when Miss Bennet added, "I must remind you that you agreed to keep my confidence. Not a word of this conversation is to reach your cousin while we mutually reside at Rosings. When we are in separate counties, you may tell him whatever you like. Mr

Darcy, I am sure, will be happy to be done with me once and for all, so it might be wiser simply to keep silent, but I shall leave that to your discretion."

The colonel liked that even less but had to admit that once again he had given his word with no idea of the costs, so he had no choice.

CHAPTER TWO

Proper Instruction

COLONEL FITZWILLIAM LED ELIZABETH DOWN THE CORRIDOR
and into the grand but garishly decorated parlour where he
said Lady Catherine liked to hold court. She stood behind him
as he called out to his aunt.

"Lady Catherine, Miss Bennet has requested a short
private conference if you do not mind."

His aunt, ensconced in an ornate chair, looked at him scep-
tically. "A private conference? I have never heard of such a
thing. What could she possibly want?"

"She is right here," he said, stepping aside to reveal Elizabeth, standing patiently to be noticed. "You may ask her yourself at your leisure."

"Do not be impertinent, Fitzwilliam."

Elizabeth noted the colonel was enjoying his aunt's
discomposure. It was admittedly amusing to see a lady who so
firmly controlled everything in her house so easily rattled by
unexpected visitors. On the few occasions they had been in
company at Rosings, Lady Catherine had questioned her
relentlessly, interrupted her conversations, and lectured her on

her failings. In spite of it all, Elizabeth found herself admiring the outspoken dowager.

Lady Catherine peered closely at her. "Miss Bennet, why are you here? I assume it is a matter of some import, and I am pleased you came to me. I am most attentive to these matters."

"Your attentiveness to all matters within your purview is legendary, my lady. It never occurred to me to approach it any other way."

"How may I help you?"

"Lady Catherine, it is a very simple thing for someone of your stature—an act that provides me with numerous benefits at little trouble or expense to yourself."

Elizabeth's request appeared to please the lady. "Nephew, you may leave us. I shall see Miss Bennet safely returned to the parsonage."

"But then I shall miss—"

Elizabeth turned to him. "Thank you, sir. I must speak to your aunt in private."

"Very well. Ladies," the colonel said with a slight bow before turning to leave.

Elizabeth watched him walk out of the parlour and was surprised when Lady Catherine addressed her with narrowed eyes.

"You appear to have my nephew wrapped around your finger."

"No, ma'am. He simply agreed to help me with the small matter of arranging a private audience. I wished it done quietly, with no chance of being impolite or causing embarrassment. He and I shall never be any more than indifferent acquaintances."

"Are you certain, Miss Bennet?"

Elizabeth sighed. "You need not pretend ignorance for the

sake of politeness, my lady. Your nephew must marry with an eye to fortune, and as you well know, I have none. Let us not bandy words. I shall assert you are not a fool."

"Point taken, Miss Bennet. I think I like you." Lady Catherine gestured to a chair. "Sit down and make your appeal."

"Thank you, ma'am." Elizabeth situated herself on the uncomfortable seat and began. "I have a rather urgent need to return to town on a personal matter. My uncle planned to send a manservant and carriage for me in a fortnight, but I need to be away on the morrow. Could you oblige me by sending a maid to ride the post with me? My uncle will see her safely back to Rosings in his own carriage within a day or two, and I would be happy to pay her wages. I could ask Mr Collins to send Hannah, but I thought you might have someone more suitable, so I must depend on your counsel and generosity."

Lady Catherine stared at the young lady and tried to stifle a laugh. "Doing it a bit brown, Miss Bennet?"

Taken aback, Elizabeth stuttered out an apology. "Perhaps I may have been in my cousin's company a bit too much."

"Perhaps so. If you need instruction in brevity, you should spend more time with Darcy. He never uses five words when three will do, and those will come out after you forgot the question as he tries to get it down to two or even one with four syllables."

Elizabeth chuckled. "Fear not, my lady. With your assistance, I shall be in the company of my most sensible aunt and sister by tomorrow night, and all will be well."

"Why have you such an urgent need to go to town?"

"I cannot reveal my reasons without breaking a confidence, ma'am. I shall simply ask that you take me at my word.

If I ask too much of your trust, pray forgive me. I shall find another means of travel."

"My trust, you say. I am the most trustworthy personage in the kingdom!"

The dowager's voice held a note of pique, and Elizabeth awaited a lecture on her presumption.

Instead, Lady Catherine sniffed and waved her lace handkerchief. "I shall see you delivered safely to your uncle tomorrow with full propriety. I would wish to know the reason for your haste. This seems somewhat precipitous."

Elizabeth could in no way mention the mutual antipathy between herself and Mr Darcy. She did not want to antagonise Lady Catherine. She was Charlotte's patroness, and Elizabeth had gained a certain fondness for the mistress of Rosings.

"I cannot oblige you. I would if I could, but—"

"Have no fear, Miss Bennet. I applaud you for keeping the confidence. When will you return to Rosings?"

"I know not. I hope to visit Mrs Collins again next year. I am afraid I shall not be able to come for tea today, but I do thank you very kindly for the honour of the invitation and for your hospitality. I must pack my things and be prepared to leave."

As expected, Lady Catherine launched into quite a long dissertation on the proper way to pack gowns, and the subject was covered in such exhaustive detail that the lady called a servant for tea before she was finished. Elizabeth managed to continue the discussion for some time with a few carefully worded questions. Before long, the time they were to have met for tea had come and gone without her having to endure either of the grand lady's nephews, exactly as planned. She surprised herself by enjoying the conference and was even more amazed to learn several good ideas for keeping her gowns less wrinkled.

Finally, it came time for leave-taking. "You will be ready by ten o'clock tomorrow."

"I am in your debt, Lady Catherine. Might I ask one more favour, if it is not too much trouble?"

Lady Catherine chuckled. "Your presumption matches your sensibility, Miss Bennet. I shall accommodate you."

Elizabeth posed her request delicately. "If you would instruct Mr Collins that you are not offended by my departure, it might save me an hour of rather tedious conversation."

She was heartened by Lady Catherine's surprisingly hearty laughter. "You are an amusing sort of girl, Miss Bennet. Your request is easily done. I shall see to it."

"I thank you, my lady. You have been most kind."

The dowager waved her off with what Elizabeth thought might have been a fond look. "John will see you back to the parsonage."

Elizabeth knew better than to argue about the need for the footman's company, thanked the lady again, curtseyed, and made good her escape. She reckoned she was only sixteen hours and one awkward, half-true conversation with Charlotte away from being gone forever from the despicable Mr Darcy.

CHAPTER THREE

———•————•———

You Know Why!

THE KNOCK ON THE DOOR CAME A MOMENT BEFORE THE
parsonage's mantel clock struck ten. As expected, the previous
evening's discussion with Charlotte had been insufficient to
satisfy her friend's curiosity, but Charlotte eventually accepted
that Elizabeth had her reasons, and they would remain private.

True to her word, Lady Catherine had informed Mr Collins
of her departure with a short note, so Elizabeth was spared
more than an hour of his chattering.

Trying to ignore the pensive expression on Charlotte's
face, which seemed to indicate her friend was far from satisfied with her explanation, Elizabeth hurried to open the door
and stepped out, only to gasp in consternation.

"Mr Darcy, what are you doing here?"

It was blisteringly obvious what he was doing, but Elizabeth was so startled she blurted out the question as though she
were Lydia, showing her lack of decorum once again.

Seeing the finely polished Darcy coach, with the man
himself and Colonel Fitzwilliam standing by with horses at the
ready, was answer enough. Clearly, this was Lady Catherine's
doing. She had obviously browbeaten her nephews into deliv-

ering Elizabeth to London. Whether it was because the grand lady could not stand the idea of a Rosings guest taking the stage, or whether she was taking advantage of the gentlemen's planned departure to kill two birds with one stone was anybody's guess. Either way, Darcy's presence was unexpected and unwelcome.

Mr Darcy bowed slightly less haughtily than usual. "My aunt informed us you were going to London. I offered to deliver you since we are London-bound."

Elizabeth was exasperated. "I asked your aunt for a *maid* to ride the stage with me—*not* for a carriage. I presume you brought the maid?"

Darcy appeared perplexed by her response. "Of course! Mrs Storey was going to town to visit her daughter for her confinement. She will ride with you and return in a month. It is no trouble at all."

As the maid stepped down from the carriage and curtseyed, Elizabeth frowned, not quite sure what to say. Mrs Storey was a woman in her forties, who looked as though she brooked no nonsense. Elizabeth liked her immediately, as she did most matrons.

Elizabeth smiled. "Mrs Storey, would you mind terribly riding the stage with me?"

"That is not necessary, Miss Bennet. We brought the carriage for your comfort. Colonel Fitzwilliam and I shall ride. It will be completely proper and no trouble at all," Darcy said.

Still distressed, Elizabeth ignored his outburst and continued to look to Mrs Storey, who had been given no opportunity to answer.

"I am at your disposal, ma'am. You saved me from paying the fare myself, so I am happy to accompany you. Which coach we take makes no difference, as I would have been on the stage within the week in any case—and alone at that." She leant in and whispered, "To be honest, I prefer the stage. I do not have to worry about dirtying such fine equipage."

"You and I shall do very well together. I have the tickets already, and my cousin has arranged a cart. Have you any baggage?"

Darcy, feeling thoroughly ignored—for quite possibly the first time in his life—decided to intervene once again.

"I repeat, Miss Bennet, our intent is for you to ride in my coach."

"That is not necessary. I have arrangements that perfectly satisfy my needs. I shall write your aunt on my arrival, expressing my pleasure with her assistance. You may go about your business."

Darcy growled in frustration. "My *business* for the day is delivering you safely to London."

Elizabeth smiled. "Which duty you have discharged admirably! Mrs Storey and I shall do quite well. Your aunt cannot fault you in the least. All is as it should be."

Darcy felt as though there was some conversation going on he could not understand. To be honest, anybody preferring the stage to the Darcy coach would have to be addle-headed, so he reckoned there was something occurring beneath the surface, something beyond his comprehension. Of course, since he was a man talking to a woman, having something beyond his understanding was not unusual. He thought to try once more to grasp the situation.

"You must understand it is not the slightest trouble or

inconvenience to deliver you safely. The coach will go to London with or without you. Mrs Storey will go to London. The colonel and I shall ride regardless. There will be no impropriety. I do not understand your reticence."

She was still standing beside Mrs Storey, so Elizabeth stepped closer to the gentleman and spoke softly.

"You do not seem to understand what I am saying. I do not need a ride to town. I only need accompaniment."

"And you seem to be operating under the mistaken belief this is a burden. I am more than happy to see you safely delivered," he replied with a huff of frustration.

"Yes, I understand I *could* ride in your coach, but I *will* not."

Darcy shook his head. He started to speak two or three times but stopped himself each time.

Instead of belabouring her point, Elizabeth lowered her voice again so only Darcy could hear. "You know why I cannot accept your offer. I ask only that you do the gentlemanly thing, and refrain from forcing me to state the reason explicitly."

At an impasse, he simply bowed. "I wish you a pleasant journey, Miss Bennet."

Elizabeth stepped back and curtseyed to both gentlemen. "Mr Darcy, Colonel Fitzwilliam...I wish you good fortune. Good-bye!"

Colonel Fitzwilliam had a difficult time deciding whether to be concerned by Darcy's abject confusion or to enjoy his cousin's misery for a while. The man was completely befuddled by Miss Bennet's rejection of his coach, and if the colonel was to keep his word, his cousin was to remain ignorant for some time.

They both watched the lady curtsey and walk away, wishing them good fortune with a tone of voice that indicated that by good fortune she meant 'much pestilence'. The colonel could only imagine the lady's true thoughts.

He had been trying for the last half a day to unravel the story of his cousin and Miss Bennet with nothing much to show for it. He had not been there to witness the beginning or the middle. He could only rely on the evidence of the two principals' interactions at Rosings and second-hand reports of their time in Hertfordshire. He felt as though he had to commit his troops to battle with no intelligence but three scouts, all drunk, delivering contradictory reports. Even the fact that he had survived that exact situation more than once was not helpful, though.

The colonel had tried every theory he could think of to explain Miss Bennet's conversation, up to and including the most radical he could imagine: that Darcy was in love with Miss Bennet but too tongue-tied to do anything about it. Of course, that did not explain Miss Bennet's report that Darcy had insulted her more than once or that they constantly argued. That did not sound very much like love at all, so the colonel abandoned that theory almost immediately.

He, of course, had no trouble understanding Miss Bennet's reluctance to use Darcy's carriage. If she esteemed her sister as much as she claimed, the only surprise was that she did not ask Lady Catherine for the loan of a large footman to beat Darcy senseless.

He smiled in amusement. "That was interesting!"

Darcy looked around and scowled in complete perplexity.

"What could she mean? She asserts I should understand her reluctance, but her estimation of my perspicuity seems wildly optimistic. I do not understand at all."

Still bound by his oath, Colonel Fitzwilliam offered a sensible explanation, hoping it might compel Darcy to admit to the Bingley predicament.

"Perhaps she has a matchmaking mother or gossipy neighbours and does not wish to excite rumours. A lady's reputation is more fragile than we think."

"Yes, she does have a violently mercenary mother, I must admit."

"Do you refer to Anne or Miss Bennet?"

Darcy's head shot up to stare at his cousin, but he seemed to lack a quick rejoinder. Instead, he only stared with a pensive frown and grunted. "I admit your supposition makes sense, but blast it! How could a simple carriage ride—"

"How indeed?" the colonel asked, wondering exactly what happened in Hertfordshire. "Come, Darcy! Let us head towards town. Miss Bennet should be on her way within half an hour. When we get to Bromley, we can take a meal and ensure she safely transfers without her knowledge. It seems the minimally gentlemanly thing to do."

Still bewildered but unwilling to let Miss Bennet completely escape his inadequate protection, Darcy agreed. He was tempted to buy a ticket himself, but that would be a far worse offence than riding beside his own coach. Miss Bennet had made her disinclination for close proximity clear enough. He imagined that with a mother like hers, she could not be too careful. With a sigh, he instructed his coachman to meet them at Bromley and was off.

Mired as he was in confusion and frustration over Miss Bennet's sudden leave-taking, Darcy was grateful for the relative peace of the journey. The two cousins shared a bit of desultory conversation on the trip, but the difficulty of talking while riding on a heavily travelled road limited their remarks.

They finally arrived at the station, made familiar by their years of visits to Rosings as a stop to change horses or refresh themselves. They climbed down, and after ascertaining that the Darcy coach had been removed from sight, they asked a groom to see to their mounts' care, dusted off their trousers, and entered a nearby tavern

They took a private room overlooking the street, and the colonel quickly ordered a meal and a bottle of brandy.

Darcy looked askance as they rarely indulged in more than wine with a meal, especially when they had more riding to do.

"Take my word, Cousin. You want the liquor."

"May I ask why?"

The colonel shrugged.

"Do you plan to stop being so blasted mysterious anytime soon, Richard?" Darcy snapped.

"In about an hour."

Darcy rolled his eyes. The meal came, and the men had just finished, talking of nothing of importance until they saw the stage arrive.

They both watched keenly out the window as Miss Bennet and Mrs Storey exited to walk around in the yard for a few minutes, chatting amiably.

Stages made quick work of changes. Darcy had seen it done in less than five minutes, and exceeding fifteen was a very bad show. Passengers were expected to be on board, or they were simply left behind, so they were not allowed to wander far.

True to their craft, a mere ten minutes later, the stage sped off. Both men assessed the fellow passengers and found nothing of any particular concern.

The colonel poured out two more glasses of brandy. "Drink up, old man." Then he pulled out his watch to note the time. "How far to the county line? Two miles?"

Darcy had no reason to believe the county line had moved recently, and his cousin knew exactly where it was. The question seemed rhetorical. "Yes, two miles."

"So that coach will cross it in twenty minutes."

"What the devil are you about?" Darcy asked, his exasperation increasing by the second.

"Miss Bennet asked me to keep a confidence as long as we were in the same county."

Darcy laughed. "So, if we had gone in the coach or rode ahead?"

"I suppose we could have ridden through Middlesex and into Hertfordshire, but I wanted to be sure she made this transfer." He smirked. "I also thought some fortification might be in order."

"Has it been twenty minutes yet? Can we abandon this ridiculous—"

The colonel slapped the table. "Do not finish that sentence. I gave my word."

Darcy followed the suggestion and took a few more sips of his brandy until the colonel snapped his watch shut.

"That should do it."

"What is this about?"

The colonel took a fortifying breath. "Why do you dislike Miss Bennet? What offence did she commit?"

Darcy stared at him like an idiot for several seconds, evidently unable to evaluate the question, so the colonel continued. "More importantly, what in the world did Miss Bennet do to offend you enough to slight her before you were even introduced?"

Finally understanding the import of the question, Darcy answered the only way a man of sense and education could. He leant his head back in an elegant, smooth, gentlemanlike manner, lay it against the tall oak seatback, and closed his eyes.

"Nothing, truly nothing."

CHAPTER FOUR

Fresh Brandy

"I THINK WE NEED MORE BRANDY," COLONEL FITZWILLIAM said with a reasonable approximation of a serious mien.

Darcy motioned to the serving maid and looked at the colonel. "It would seem you have had some rather interesting conversations with Miss Bennet."

"Indeed, I have. She makes a convincing case that you dislike her badly enough to rip Bingley away from her favourite sister—not that the ability to steer Bingley is anything to boast about."

"I take your point. He is somewhat easily led, and I admit to discouraging him from pursuing Miss Bennet, but he is a grown man who makes his own decisions." Darcy levelled a serious look at his overly amused cousin. "However, that is not the most shocking thing. What exactly did you say to her to instigate a conversation about my supposed dislike of her?"

Fitzwilliam chuckled. "Avoiding the question?"

"*Deferring!* May we start at the beginning."

The colonel settled back in his chair, a more sober expression on his face. "When Miss Bennet mentioned Georgiana, I was alarmed that she might have heard something of—"

Darcy flushed in anger. "If she did, it could only be from one source."

"Wickham! Do you know where he is?"

"Hertfordshire. He joined the militia and is spreading his usual lies."

"You corrected them though, did you not?"

Darcy did not reply, mindful that his cousin was growing more agitated but too angry with Wickham and with himself to respond.

"Did you warn the townspeople at least?" When his cousin did not answer, Fitzwilliam snorted in disgust. "You did not."

"No, I did not! I was otherwise occupied, and I cannot follow that villain around, correcting every mistaken impression. I was worried about Georgie's reputation."

George Wickham was a vile reprobate, but bringing him to heel without damaging Georgiana's reputation required harsher measures than either man was willing to countenance. Darcy knew the colonel would have been happy just to kill him, but he was too shocked by that which had nearly befallen his sister; he cared only that the man could no longer threaten her or her reputation and thus allowed Wickham to move his depredations from one town to another. *A grievous mistake,* Darcy thought, rubbing his face.

"Surely, you warned Miss Elizabeth, at least."

Darcy groaned. "I told her only that Wickham is capable of making friends but unlikely to keep them."

His cousin's look of disbelief prompted Darcy to justify himself. "She asked me in the middle of a dance at a ball. I was unwilling to lay out my concerns publicly, and I was afraid of singling her out, raising expectations, or starting gossip. As a second son, you have no idea how easy it is to get leg shackled or damage a woman's reputation."

The colonel snorted in disapproval. "Yes, I understand you deplore my lack of candour, but shall we continue? She spoke of Georgiana?"

"I mentioned we shared guardianship of her, and she asked if she gave us much trouble. It appears much of what she thought she knew of Georgiana consisted of Miss Bingley's blathering. She knew nothing ill of her but understands that trouble is almost universally expected for fifteen-year-old girls."

Darcy felt some relief. "Miss Bennet is the second eldest of five daughters. Her youngest sister is fifteen and practically feral. Her neighbourhood has at least another half a dozen young ladies of that age, so I suppose she has some right to expertise on the matter—certainly more than you or I can claim."

"The mention of Miss Bingley led her to ask whether I knew Bingley and feeling rather boastful on your behalf, I told her you saved a friend from the inconveniences of a most imprudent marriage."

"Blast it!" Darcy reacted as any sensible man would, by leaning down and beating his head against the table. "The imprudent marriage was to Miss Bennet's much-beloved elder sister."

"Yes, she…ah…informed me."

Darcy grumbled. "I wager that was amusing. What next?"

"She indicated she was not entirely satisfied with the transaction and asked what reason you gave."

Being perfectly able to imagine what 'not entirely satisfied' meant, Darcy groaned. "And you said?"

"I understood that there were some very strong objections against the lady."

Darcy shook his head. "Worse and worse."

The colonel went on. "She was silent, probably thinking about the relative efficacy of knives versus ropes for murdering you, and finally said, 'That explains everything,' and proceeded to relate her newly discovered theory. Then, she asked me to take her to Rosings to talk to Lady Catherine. I was not privy to their conversation, but I believe she was intent on leaving so you could enjoy the rest of your stay absent her presence, or she planned to go directly to her sister to reveal your perfidy. I knew she was serious, but I was sworn to silence, so here we are."

Darcy moaned. "Yes, here we are."

They sat staring at the table, unable to look at each other for quite some time, occasionally taking a sip of brandy.

Finally, Fitzwilliam asked, "Any truth to her theory that you hate her?"

Darcy looked him in the eye. "That, my friend, is as far from the truth as possible."

"You are in love with her?"

The disbelief in his cousin's voice only worsened Darcy's misery. "Yes, and I naturally made a complete hash of it."

"Well, they say love and hate are two sides of the same coin. Maybe Miss Bennet just looked at the wrong side."

"You are quite the philosopher, Richard," Darcy said drily as he sat, sipping his drink slowly, trying not to think about the disaster he had created for himself.

"Instead of sulking, tell me the whole story."

Darcy shook his head in resignation and began. "It all started at an assembly. You can imagine my usual attitude in such a place."

"You are not the most sociable man I know."

"You had been tending to your duties since summer. I had been tending to my sister, and it had not been going well. Your mother finally had enough and told me to go to Hertfordshire to help Bingley, go to Pemberley, go to the Continent, go anywhere else so Georgiana and I would quit feeding each other's misery."

"It does not sound very appealing."

"No. It was sensible though, so I took her advice. Then, through a spectacular failure of luck and planning, I spent a four-hour carriage ride with Miss Bingley and Mrs Hurst."

The colonel leant over and rapped the side of his head with his fist to display proper manly sympathy with such disagreeable company. "Fate worse than death."

"It gets worse. Bingley accepted an invitation to an assembly the same night, less than four hours after we arrived." Darcy stared into his glass. "You know how I detest those things! Five minutes in and all you could hear were whispers of 'ten thousand a year' and all the usual things that go with a large income and matchmaking mamas."

The colonel let out a most indecorous guffaw. "Carry on, my good man. I assume some squire dragged you around for introductions."

"Yes! He started with the Bennets. The eldest two are polite and well mannered. The rest are … not. Of course, I did not see that immediately. Bingley was introduced to the three eldest and the mother. Mr Bennet was not in attendance. Bingley declared the eldest to be an angel. I could predict he would take up with her from five paces—which he did at the first opportunity."

"Like a clock, that one. I assume you employed your usual compromise avoidance strategy."

"You like to tease me about it, but it has been tried—more than once. I learnt that lesson the hard way. I would wager you learnt to dig in the first time a bullet missed you by a foot."

The colonel nodded sagely. "What next?"

Darcy drained the remainder of his brandy and poured another—probably not the wisest notion of the afternoon. "Then, my friend, the story of Mr Fitzwilliam Darcy and Miss Elizabeth Bennet began in earnest."

After Darcy completed telling the entire tale of their interactions in Hertfordshire, the colonel leant back and stared pensively at him.

"So, the entire time you were in Hertfordshire, you danced with exactly one lady, and even that, you managed to turn into an argument."

"I always want to ensure I do not create expectations."

Colonel Fitzwilliam chuckled. "In that, my friend, you succeeded admirably."

"You do not have to enjoy my misery so much."

"On the contrary, I am excessively compelled to enjoy every minute of it. I consider it part of my duty to King and Country."

A few more growls and frowns from Darcy proved sufficient to quiet his companion, and they sat in silence.

The colonel finally asked, "Tell me about your time with her in Kent—the parts I did not see."

Darcy explained their few walks and had to admit that Elizabeth seemed more confused than anything.

Fitzwilliam chuckled. "It is not puzzling at all. I imagine she told you it was a favourite walk so you could avoid it, not ambush her. If she held to her previous assumption that you shared—how did she put it—a 'rather mild mutual antipathy,' then your behaviour would have been truly baffling. I imagine if you implied that she might be staying at Rosings, she may have thought you were hinting about an attachment to me."

Darcy gasped, feeling his heart pound in his chest at the idea.

"Steady on, man! I doubt very much she had any interest in me. She talked to me because I am the only member of the party who was willing and able to speak sensibly. She was in company with that ridiculous parson, our overbearing aunt, and my silent-as-a-tomb cousin—nay cousins. What choice did she have?"

They sat for another hour, talking and drinking, before climbing unsteadily into the carriage for the last leg of the journey. Darcy, morose and far more in his cups than customary, was about to fall asleep when his cousin roused him with a slap on the knee.

"Darcy, you must tell this entire story to Georgiana."

Oh yes, I must share my mortification with my younger sister! Perfect idea. Instead of the harangue his cousin deserved for such an idiotic suggestion, Darcy simply asked, "Why?"

"I believe it will aid her recovery from the events of last summer."

"How so?"

"It will do her a world of good to be promoted to the second stupidest Darcy."

CHAPTER FIVE

•———•

Punishment

FITZWILLIAM DARCY AWOKE TO WHAT COULD ONLY BE described as torture—absolute, sheer, deliberate torture.

On this, of all days, his sister felt the need to practise chromatic scales. Naturally, she decided to do it in the upstairs music room, which was only two doors from his chambers, and apparently, Thursday was *fortissimo* day. The same tedious thirty-six notes up and down, over and over and over and over.

With a frightening scream, Darcy yelled at the top of his lungs and got out of bed. The fact that he landed on the floor on his backside instead of his feet hardly signified. However, the scream did the trick and silenced the pianoforte—for about a minute.

Feeling as though the world had ended, an assertion not quite as hyperbolic as it seemed, he climbed to his feet and rang for his man, Bates.

As he had the evening before, Bates showed no sign of mirth at his employer's predicament and so was able to help Darcy to his bath with a straight face. He also administered a vile tasting concoction that lacked any medicinal properties whatsoever, but Darcy, like most men, associated vile taste with effectiveness and could not be convinced otherwise.

The potion, followed by a leisurely shave, was enough to make Darcy's head pound just a bit less, and he even managed to greet his sister and ask her to practise something else— anything else, somewhere else—in the nicest possible manner.

If Georgiana suspected the reason behind his headache, she said nothing. Being the most agreeable of sisters, she left Darcy alone throughout the rest of the day and even let him go to bed unmolested.

Her forbearance, however, ended the next morning after breakfast when she followed Darcy into his study and curled up in the chair across from his desk. He smiled at her, a little concerned at the unexpected intrusion.

"Brother, when you were in trouble as a boy, how did you feel after Father punished you for some transgression?"

"What do you mean?" Darcy asked in genuine confusion. He had his duty impressed on him since before he could properly talk, so his punishments had come as the result of Wickham's deeds far more often than his own. In an instant, the answer came to him abruptly. Feeling chagrined, he muttered, "I felt relieved."

"Why?"

Darcy had to think about it. In truth, any punishment he received never took long. The most protracted lecture he might endure was an hour—less than his shortest conversation with Lady Catherine. If his father decided to apply a belt or rod, it would be over in a matter of minutes. Neither event weighed heavily.

"Because it was over. Father assumed the punishment had done its job, and he did not bring up that infraction again."

Georgiana nodded solemnly. "I believe our father was a

fair man and did not dwell on transgressions. The deed was done. Responsibility was assigned. Consequences were meted out. He was satisfied."

Darcy sat back, impressed. "You are far more thoughtful than I realised. More thoughtful than I am, to be honest."

She shrugged. "You have an estate to run, Fitzwilliam. I have few responsibilities. For the last half a year, I have spent my time being miserable and playing the pianoforte. I love the instrument, and I own I am quite good, but the truth is that I spend so much time practicing because it distracts me from my thoughts."

The guilt Darcy felt at her words must have shown on his face, for Georgiana quickly went on.

"I do not say this in censure. You were thrust into an untenable situation. You gained control of an estate and a sister all at the same time. Before that, you hardly ever saw me. For most of my life, you were at Eton and Cambridge. You did not have the advantage of seeing me grow from the start. You did not have a wife or mother to guide you, and most of the mother figures you could have picked would have been awful. You have done your best, and your best is good enough. What happened last summer was a terrible mistake, but I am stronger now."

Darcy gave his sister a small smile. "When did you become so wise, Georgie? I fear that in my conceit, I have been unwilling to admit you are growing up."

"Perhaps growing up is mostly deciding you will behave as though you are grown with the hope that others will go along."

Darcy chuckled. "I shall comply. Would it help you if I give you a thrashing or tongue-lashing?"

"If you admit to my culpability and stupidity, I shall be satisfied."

Darcy looked thoughtful. "What if I had done so last summer?"

Georgiana waited to answer for some time, and finally shrugged a bit. "I cannot know the right thing to have done months ago. It might have done me a world of good, or it might have crushed me. That said, I do know the right thing to do now."

"Which is?"

"Honest conversation. I do believe that is the cure for a multitude of problems." She paused and gave him a beseeching look. "Fitzwilliam, what happened the other night that resulted in your arriving home from Rosings thoroughly tap-hackled with my supposedly more responsible co-guardian?"

Darcy flushed, mortified that his sister had any knowledge that he and Fitzwilliam had stumbled in rather drunkenly two nights prior. Georgiana looked at him earnestly, and he took her hand in his.

"Tap-hackled, my dear? Where have you learnt such language?" He managed a smile. "You would agree with our cousin. Richard asserted that I should tell you because you would enjoy being the *second* stupidest Darcy."

"It sounds as though he said something wise for once. I suppose it was bound to happen sooner or later."

"That he did. I admit it was a frightfully embarrassing tale the first time. I have no idea if the second will be easier because of repetition or harder because I am embarrassed to expose you to my folly."

"There is another possibility you have not mentioned. I may be able to help you."

Bemused, he crossed his arms. "How?"

Georgiana leant in close. "I assume the problem is with a woman—something romantic—perhaps something to do with Hertfordshire last autumn?"

He raised one eyebrow.

"Let me ask you a question, Brother. How did you learn to be master of an estate?"

"I learnt the most important lessons by working with Father. It is true I was at Eton and Cambridge for years, but Father made sure I spent many hours riding the estate, observing him doing the master's work, and teaching me important lessons. In the end, I think it was mostly exposure."

"What do you think I have been exposed to all my life?"

Darcy had no answer.

"Women."

He startled and stared at her in surprise.

"In my cradle, I was attended by a wetnurse and nursery maid. By the time I could talk, I was surrounded by nursery maids, day and night. Later, it was nurses and governesses, then governesses and masters. They were single or married, quiet or gossipy, reticent or voluble, handsome or not. They talked to their peers about many subjects that are never taught to ladies. Then, I went to school with girls, most of whom were terribly ignorant but unrepentant gossips.

"For most of my life, men were mythical creatures, existing only in the form of ancient masters or family members. I may not know very much about men, but I can assure you I know a great deal about women."

Darcy considered what she said for a moment before breaking into a smile. "So, I have had ready access to an acknowledged expert on women right under my nose for years without even knowing it because I could not see my little sister as a woman. Ironic, no?"

Georgiana laughed as though finally seeing the humour of the situation. She called for tea. They sat chuckling and reviewing all that she had said until it arrived.

After she poured them each a cup, Darcy said, "It is time, Georgie. I hope you can save me from myself."

She smiled brightly. "Of course I can."

With that, for the second time in three days, Darcy told the story of his acquaintance with Miss Elizabeth Bennet and her family, starting from 'not handsome enough' and ending with his highly entertaining return to Darcy House with a valuable lesson in life about overindulgence.

For the rest of the morning, the siblings discussed what had been said, not said, or implied, along with Georgiana's best guesses about how the Miss Bennets probably felt and acted. It was a revelation to Darcy, gaining insight through his sister into the mind of a lady such as Elizabeth Bennet. He had no idea how it felt to be powerless, to have an entail hanging over your head, to have a critical mother, or to have to wait for a man to make a declaration.

One thing was certain. He had been terrified that his sister would be ill-equipped to come out. Now it seemed she would be well prepared. Of course, she implied with sublime subtlety, coming out with a new sister would be an improvement over coming out without one.

Georgiana proceeded to tell her brother exactly what he needed to do. She asserted that she was just reminding him of what his heart and his honour already knew, but confirmation never hurt.

Darcy spent the rest of his day mulling over his feelings and failings and considering how best to approach Elizabeth and her sister. Apologies, amends, and assistance would be required. Would that they could forgive him! First, he needed to find them. Gracechurch Street, was it?

With a lighter heart, Darcy went to bed that night, ready for the hard work ahead.

CHAPTER SIX

Forbearance

HAVING JUST RETURNED FROM A WALK, JANE AND ELIZABETH were hanging up their bonnets when their uncle's voice called out.

"Ladies, might you attend me in my study."

Elizabeth recognised the concern in his voice, similar as it was to the one he had used to greet her upon her unexpected arrival via the stage four days prior. Her decision to travel to London unannounced had not been well received, especially when she was reluctant to be explicit about why she had returned a fortnight early with only a maid for company. That conversation had not gone well at all.

Since then, the sisters had been engaged with the Gardiner family during the day, and they had spent most of their nights talking softly in their shared bedroom about all Elizabeth learnt in Kent. Between them, they had discussed everything they thought they knew, along with every wild supposition and speculation.

Jane Bennet had spent most of her life trying to find the good in everybody. Lately though, based on what Elizabeth reported—offhand comments from Lady Catherine, her conversation with Colonel Fitzwilliam, and a few brief conversations with Mr Darcy—the sisters could only conclude Miss Bingley had lied. It seemed impossible that Mr Bingley was courting Miss Darcy, so her letter was pure fabrication.

It was a fact that Mr Bingley had shown particular attention to Jane for close to two months and left Netherfield abruptly, never to return. How the blame should be apportioned between Mr Bingley, Miss Bingley, Mr Darcy, and persons unknown Elizabeth could only guess. It seemed certain someone deserved the blame for preventing Mr Bingley from taking his leave or making his lack of intentions known.

Elizabeth and her sister agreed that Mr Bingley was probably not a good enough actor to lie convincingly at the ball, so something must have persuaded him to leave Jane sometime between when he journeyed to London and when he decided never to return. Mr Darcy and Miss Bingley's interference seemed as good an explanation as any, especially since they chased him to London with far more enthusiasm than the Bennet hounds ever showed in a hunt.

It was now time to put their ruminations aside and attend Mr Gardiner.

"Of course, we shall come at once, Uncle," Jane politely answered, and the ladies repaired to the study.

Once they were seated, Mr Gardiner began. "Lizzy, I have refrained—just barely at my wife's suggestion—from asking you about what happened in Kent. However, I now believe I may have been remiss. Did anything happen that you would prefer I did not know, but you must admit I should?"

Elizabeth paled. It was obvious her uncle was worried there may have been some sort of assignation, that a man had importuned her, or any of the other hundred things he could worry about. She had refrained from discussing what happened at Rosings not because she thought her uncle would think ill of her, but because she was embarrassed. She was embarrassed by her mother and sisters' behaviour as well as her father's. Worst of all, she was embarrassed by her own.

She had let her wounded pride cause her to provoke Mr Darcy endlessly, simply because he had wounded her vanity. Her actions may well have cost Jane her happiness. Logic said her mother and sisters had a large portion of the blame, but Elizabeth was convinced she was the one most culpable.

She straightened her spine and began to explain. "You know that Mr Darcy and I share a long-standing mutual antagonism."

Mr Gardiner gave a small nod.

"I learnt in Kent from a reliable source that Mr Darcy saved a friend from the inconveniences of a most imprudent marriage. I learnt the friend was Mr Bingley, and the imprudent marriage would have been to Jane. This information added to my belief that Mr Darcy must hate my family in general and me in particular. I decided to be polite and leave his company at Rosings, so I took the stage to save us both further embarrassment."

Eyebrows raised, Uncle Gardiner asked, "Is that the only option you had?"

Elizabeth was chagrined. "I asked Lady Catherine to lend me a maid for the journey, but she apparently coerced Mr Darcy into offering his coach. I refused of course, and here we are."

"Why refuse? I cannot believe his carriage was in any way deficient, or he was trying to importune you."

"Of course not!" she said, somewhat alarmed. "It is the finest carriage I ever saw. Mr Darcy and the colonel planned to ride, but..." Elizabeth sighed. "I did not want to suffer his presence. I had heard all the words I ever wanted to hear from the man, and I found riding in his coach for four hours an unpleasant prospect. Even if he and the colonel rode, they would have been obligated to offer us refreshment in Bromley and to share conversation. Then they would have had to deliver me here. Mr Darcy may perhaps have heard of such a place as Gracechurch Street, but he would hardly think a month's ablution enough to cleanse him from its impurities, were he once to enter it." Elizabeth blanched at her uncle's disapproving frown.

"Is that fact or supposition, Lizzy?"

"Mostly supposition," she replied sheepishly. "It is not something I concocted. Rather, it is based on conversations overheard at Netherfield."

"Is that all?"

Elizabeth stared at her boots. "Can you imagine the cater-wauling if Mama discovered I had ridden from Kent to London in Mr Darcy's coach? She is still carrying on about Mr Bingley and Mr Collins. Such a thing cannot be kept secret. Besides that," Elizabeth said, twisting her hands, not at all certain, "once I knew Mr Darcy had helped break Jane's heart and then boasted about it to his cousin, I did not think I could be civil. I expect never to see the man again, and there is no point in borrowing trouble."

Gardiner was silent for a time. "What say you, Jane? You are one of the principal actors in this drama."

"While I was somewhat distressed by Lizzy taking the stage, I admit that avoiding Mr Darcy was very much to my liking, Uncle."

"I see. Do you concur with Lizzy's theory that Mr Darcy hates us?"

Jane looked pained. "It is the only theory we can come up with that makes any sense. We differ only in particulars."

"How so?"

"Lizzy believes herself the principal architect of my doom because she teased and argued with Mr Darcy after he wounded her vanity with some unkind remarks before they were introduced. I think she just enjoys being thought the worst person in the world, which I fear is an example of unregulated pride."

"Unregulated pride?" Elizabeth gasped in consternation, but she did not have the heart to argue.

"You like to take the blame, but do you really believe you can compete with our mother, Lizzy? She talked ceaselessly and loudly about how Mr Bingley was as much as secured, and the only question remaining was the date for our wedding. Think of the behaviour of Lydia and Kitty in company, or Mary's performance on the pianoforte, or—"

Elizabeth laughed and held up a hand. "Peace! Peace, Jane! I shall admit I may not carry all the blame."

"Ladies, I can only imagine the things that went on at the ball."

"That is probably for the best. It was truly awful, and I think I am still red from embarrassment to this day. I am not certain I blame Mr Bingley for anything other than his failure to take his leave or clearly state his intentions or lack thereof."

Elizabeth paused before saying, "Is that all, Uncle?"

"Not quite." He leant back in his chair, tapping his finger on his chin. "I have received an unusual and rather unorthodox request. I wanted to know the lay of the land before I allow or deny it."

Elizabeth glanced at Jane and saw her equally curious.

Both ladies looked at him warily but did not respond, since their uncle seemed deep in thought.

Eventually, with a look of resolve, he leant forward. "I shall allow it, I think."

"Allow what, exactly, sir?" Jane asked.

"I have a gentleman in the parlour who would like to speak to the both of you in private. He says he owes each of you an apology and begs leave to have a private discussion."

Elizabeth gasped. "How is this proper?"

"You will act as mutual chaperons, so only you two will be privy to what is said. It is a bit unconventional, I admit, but I shall leave the door open and remain close by."

Always aware of the fragility of her reputation, Elizabeth had a natural aversion to private conversations, yet she burned with curiosity.

A gentleman *wishing* to apologise? Mr Bingley was the only man she could think of that could and should apologise to both sisters, but she judged his willingness to stand up to Uncle Gardiner's scrutiny unlikely. Colonel Fitzwilliam seemed a much more reasonable candidate. Elizabeth could imagine his chagrin at being taken to task by Mr Darcy for his unguarded gossiping on her last day in Kent.

She felt Jane's imploring gaze and gave her hand a reassuring squeeze before speaking to her uncle. "We trust your judgment. We shall meet this gentleman, but it would be helpful if we had some idea who he is and why he is here."

Mr Gardiner rose from his desk with renewed energy. "Come along, now," he said without even pretending to answer the question.

As the ladies followed him into the parlour, he said, "Here they are, Mr Darcy. I shall allow this only once. I expect complete decorum. Do not test my forbearance."

CHAPTER SEVEN

Apologies

"Miss Bennet, Miss Elizabeth, I thank you for seeing me."

Even though I suspect you would rather not, Darcy thought as he bowed. Determined to make amends and beg their pardon, he was prepared for their anger, their annoyance, and even their tears.

The sisters curtseyed and murmured, "Mr Darcy."

There was a moment of awkward silence until Mr Gardiner spoke. "I shall retreat to my study across the hall and leave both doors open. If you refrain from shouting or breaking things, your conversation will remain reasonably private."

With that statement and a slight smirk that reminded Darcy of Mr Bennet, Mr Gardiner bowed and quit the room. The trio remained standing until Elizabeth appeared to recall her manners.

"May we call for refreshments, Mr Darcy?"

"Not at present. I thank you."

Jane asked, "Will you sit, sir?"

The ladies shared a sofa, while Darcy sat in a leather

armchair facing them. Elizabeth looked at him curiously, while her sister wore her usual veil of impassive serenity.

Darcy did not expect this interview to be easy. "Ladies, I have come to offer some very belated apologies," he said gravely, hoping to impress them with his sincerity,

Jane looked confused. "Apologies, Mr Darcy?"

"Can you be more specific?" Elizabeth asked.

"I owe one to each of you individually and one to both of you collectively." He paused a moment and shook his head. "I do not quite know where to begin."

Jane took pity on him. "I find any organisation superior to none. We have all day, so it does not signify if you present in the best way or not. Perhaps it would be best to start at the beginning."

"Perhaps not the beginning, but I can start with a beginning."

"That will do nicely, sir," she said as kindly as she could manage, considering how angry she was with him.

Darcy turned towards her sister. "Miss Elizabeth, on the first evening of our acquaintance, I slighted you. I said things a true gentleman would not even think, let alone say. What I said was both ungentlemanly and demonstrably untrue, since you are in fact one of the handsomest women of my acquaintance. I am very sorry."

He watched to see how his words affected her. She appeared startled at first and then thoughtful. The apology was well done and would have been entirely sufficient if he had not followed that slight with several other offences.

After a few moments, Elizabeth replied, "I accept your apology, and I shall try to forgive you… eventually."

He grimaced. "I am under no illusions that a simple apology will resolve the matter in my favour, Miss Elizabeth, but it is a beginning. I have other things I would like to say after I address the next two topics, but that is at least a start."

"Very well, but may I ask you something?"

"Anything."

"I would not recommend *carte blanche*, Mr Darcy," Elizabeth said archly.

Darcy smiled awkwardly, quietly thrilled by her show of impertinence. "I am still not afraid of you."

Elizabeth laughed for a moment before asking much more pensively, "Is that the only disparaging thing you said about me?"

He looked even more chagrined. "Regretfully, no. Among the Netherfield party, you well know that disparagement of the neighbourhood was rife. I did express some unkind thoughts and said things that are beneath the conduct of a gentleman. I also allowed others to speak similarly in my presence without challenge."

Mr Darcy's presence at Gracechurch Street had been astonishing, but that he had come to humble himself and offer apologies for his conduct seemed unimaginable to Elizabeth. She wondered at the reasons for his present behaviour, and all she could think of was that Colonel Fitzwilliam must have taken the man to task. No other explanation made any sense.

Uncle Gardiner had a saying: forgiveness is cheap, but it is not free. He usually meant it was best to forgive when it was possible but to be wary of the possibility of repeated transgressions. With Jane or Mary, Elizabeth could forgive and forget. Forgiving Lydia, she found more difficult. She wondered what cost she should extract from Mr Darcy and decided it was usually best to err on the side of generosity.

She took a deep breath. "I forgive you, Mr Darcy. I admit that I made light of your words at the time, but they stung. Can you tell me why you said such things?"

He looked at her somewhat intensely. "There was no real superiority of mind."

Elizabeth frowned a bit at the remembrance, unsure whether Mr Darcy was demonstrating respect for her memory or arrogance, since he obviously assumed she remembered their discussion six months prior in Netherfield's drawing room. Perhaps he assumed since she moved in a confined and unvarying society in Meryton, she would remember almost every conversation she had with an outsider—a conjecture that was unfortunately mostly true.

The thought was followed quickly by a bout of shame. The man had journeyed to Cheapside to apologise, and she still treated him as though he had no redeeming qualities at all.

"You are saying your pride was not under good regulation," she murmured.

Much to her surprise, the gentleman laughed aloud. "Running rampant would be closer to the truth."

Elizabeth had to join him. "Shall we just forgive all those slights? They are behind us now."

"Forgive, but not forget, Miss Elizabeth. I presume that behaviour gave you an unfavourable view of me, one which I perfectly well deserved."

"What do you think?" she asked with an arch of her eyebrow.

He did not answer her question but merely nodded. "That brings me to a shared apology."

Elizabeth gazed at him. Mr Darcy was handsome when he

was not frowning or sneering, and she was abashed as to how much she was enjoying their repartee.

Surprise after surprise, she thought.

Jane, who had been watching the conversation silently, spoke up. "I suppose this shared apology has something to do with Mr Wickham."

Darcy shifted his gaze to her. "It does. How did you know?"

"His presence altered you from a somewhat imperious neighbour to a truly villainous man in Lizzy's mind."

Elizabeth shifted uncomfortably. "Jane, I am not certain I used those words."

Her sister shrugged. "Perhaps not those exact words, but things changed after you met Mr Wickham. You unwisely asked Mr Darcy about him at the ball, and the company left a few hours later. I think there must be a connexion of some sort."

"May I guess, Miss Elizabeth? Did Wickham say we grew up together—played together as boys?"

"Yes," she said, somewhat cautiously.

"I shall further assume he was all praise to my good father and implied that I am not the honourable man he was?"

"Yes," she replied, slightly nervous.

"Probably claimed I denied him a living my father left to him in his will?" Darcy asked, almost in a whisper.

Elizabeth nodded in reply, wondering where this conversation was going and not liking where it had travelled so far.

"The usual lies, as expected," he said with some exasperation. "That brings me to my next apology. This is to you both, as well as to your sisters and the neighbourhood."

Darcy looked at them with an expression Elizabeth could not interpret. He began the story of the vile, cheating, reprehensible Mr Wickham and his misbehaviours, petty cruelties, debts, and dishonour.

Jane grasped Elizabeth's hand so tightly it was painful. It was a fantastic tale, yet aside from Mr Darcy coming to Cheapside and laying his soul bare, his story was completely sensible and consistent. It also pointed out several glaring inconsistencies in Mr Wickham's tale that Elizabeth should have seen from the beginning. The fact that Mr Darcy offered the testimony of Colonel Fitzwilliam as well as written receipts was entirely unnecessary. Elizabeth believed every word of it.

Jane spoke for them both. "I believe we may take you at your word, sir. We shall not need the colonel's testimony. Might you tell us why you did not warn us about Mr Wickham?"

The pain that flashed across his countenance startled Elizabeth, who remained stunned by the revelations about Mr Wickham. She wondered if he regretted not warning them or regretted the reasons behind his failure to do so.

Mr Darcy leant closer to them, and in a quiet voice began to tell them of the events of the previous summer, up to and including Georgiana's near disgrace in Ramsgate.

Jane was openly crying by the time he finished, and Elizabeth was close to it. Both ladies asked after Miss Darcy's recovery and were pleasantly surprised by the gentleman's expressing a desire to introduce his sister.

Looking exhausted, Jane asked, "Shall we take a rest to have some tea now, Mr Darcy?"

"That would be lovely."

Jane rang for the tea, and they got up from their chairs gingerly to stretch after the intensity of the conversation.

"With regard to Mr Wickham, that explains everything. I

understand why you would worry more about your sister's reputation than our neighbourhood. You are a good brother and guardian to her," Elizabeth said.

"There is no excuse aside from my conceit not to protect other young women and the local merchants. With your permission, I shall go to Meryton and warn its people about him."

Jane suddenly gasped. "Father is considering allowing Lydia to go to Brighton with Colonel Forster's wife. We must prevent it."

Mr Darcy agreed. "I have been to Brighton. I would not allow my sister or any young lady within fifty miles when the regiments are there."

Silence fell as they awaited their tea. Elizabeth wished, rather than believed, that the hardest part of the conversation was in the past.

CHAPTER EIGHT

•●————————————●••

Explanations

THE ARRIVAL OF TEA SEEMED TO PUT THE COMPANY IN A sombre mood, and after some inane conversation about travelling, Jane finally settled on something she hoped might lift their spirits. "Tell us more about your sister, Mr Darcy."

He looked like a man who had just been given a reprieve. "Georgiana is sixteen and has had the ill fortune these past five years of having myself and my cousin Colonel Fitzwilliam as her guardians. I believe Miss Elizabeth can attest to our unsuitability."

"I can assure you that the most prized skill for a gentlewoman is gossip, and with the colonel's tutelage, she should…" Elizabeth's impertinent reply died on her lips as she recognised the deeper meaning of Mr Darcy's words: he and his young sister were alone in the world, and she had slipped from impertinence nearly to cruelty.

Mr Darcy leant forward. "Although in possession of superb skill in conversation, which I must admit I envy, my cousin lacks common sense discretion, so we have given her a course of study with Miss Bingley."

Elizabeth stared at him stunned, trying to work out if he

was joking, teasing, or serious. The idea that he might tease would never have occurred to her before that afternoon, but this was… wonderfully unexpected.

While Elizabeth was trying to decide how to resolve her complete confusion, Jane saved her the trouble by starting to chuckle. Darcy joined her not much later, and Elizabeth eventually took part, finding that Darcy was in fact capable of humour. Thinking back to her conversations at Netherfield, she thought she saw instances of dry and subtly humourous remarks that she might have enjoyed if she had not been so implacably opposed to him.

It all made her wonder. Without that initial insult at the assembly, how would she have seen Mr Darcy? By his own testimony, he did not think much of the neighbourhood, so it was unlikely they would have fared much better.

However, the few times she caught him with his guard down, he had slipped some things into conversation that obviously went by both Miss Bingley and herself. For example, his comment about *extensive* reading had been a subtle rebuke of Miss Bingley, indicating she was not an accomplished woman. The comment rolled off that lady like water off a duck and escaped Elizabeth's understanding almost as quickly.

She eyed the gentleman. He obviously did not hate her as she had surmised, but with a shake of her head, Elizabeth decided she would not work it out on her own.

"Shall we proceed, Mr Darcy?" she finally said, mostly because she was tired of being confused by his behaviour, which was quite amiable at that moment. It was most surprising.

Darcy looked carefully at Miss Bennet. "I fear my biggest apology must go to you—both because the offence was the most egregious and the effects the severest."

"What have you done, Mr Darcy?" Jane asked with a surprisingly hard edge to her voice.

Darcy strongly suspected she knew exactly why he needed to apologise. She was obviously making him earn her acceptance the hard way, which was just and natural. He was not certain he would listen to any explanation if their positions were reversed. He drew a deep breath, hoped his words would draw anger rather than tears, and began.

"As Colonel Fitzwilliam informed your sister, I assisted in separating Mr Bingley from you. Although it was done in the service of a friend, it was badly done and not my place."

Darcy carried on without displaying emotion. "Sir William interrupted my dance with Miss Elizabeth at the ball to relay the gossip that most of the neighbourhood expected Bingley to make you an offer."

Elizabeth spoke sharply. "You cannot assert it was an unreasonable assumption. Mr Bingley had shown very particular attention to Jane for quite some time and was excessively attentive at the ball."

Darcy noted the hostility in the remark. "You are correct. I am not *justifying* Bingley's actions, nor my own. I am trying to *explain* them. To be honest, I had not paid much attention to the pair, but when I became aware that expectations were being raised, I took it upon myself to evaluate the situation rationally. I spent the rest of the evening watching Miss Bennet carefully. It pains me to say this, but you would not be the first woman Bingley fell half in love with overnight. Most were in town and most were quite mercenary. They usually showed their true stripes before long. You, however…"

Jane Bennet spoke icily. "I, however *what*? Explain your-self, sir!"

Darcy paled, overly conscious of how far he had gone in speaking so openly to two ladies of such short acquaintance. *Recounting their faults to their faces!*

He softened his voice and began again. "You were not of that ilk, Miss Bennet. I observed you most carefully for the rest of the ball. Your look and manners were open, cheerful, and engaging as ever, but without any symptom of peculiar regard. Thus, I remained convinced from the evening's scru-tiny that although you received Bingley's attentions with plea-sure, you did not invite them by any participation of sentiment. I shall not scruple to assert that the serenity of your countenance and air was such as might have given the most acute observer a conviction that however amiable your temper, your heart was not likely to be easily touched."

He saw Elizabeth gripping her sister's hands tightly as though to restrain herself from throttling him.

"I see! You observed Jane most carefully for all of three or four hours, and you remained convinced from the evening's scrutiny that Jane's behaviour was demure and proper as ladies are taught. She did not bandy her feelings around for the general populace, saving them for her suitor, and even then, only after he showed his interest and in rela-tive privacy. In other words, she acted in a completely lady-like manner."

"Had I shown Mr Bingley obvious favour, might you have thought me mercenary?" Jane said quietly but with growing anger on her face.

Darcy swallowed a lump in his throat at the implication, but he had to admit that acting similar to Miss Bingley would not have impressed him any more than what he had observed.

He wondered whether he was digging his hole deeper and deeper. "I suppose ladies must walk a very narrow path."

Jane protested angrily and vigorously. "I had no idea that you too were judging me, sir. Every hour of every day, I must try to please and pay heed to my mother, my father, my suitor, the neighbourhood gossips, and the rules of propriety—all while being completely unaware that I had to please you as well! Show too much affection and I am forward. Show too little and I am mercenary. You really do take on too much, sir. The path is not narrow. It is non-existent!"

Darcy stared at the floor in shame before looking Jane in the eye and continuing. "That, Miss Bennet, is precisely why I am here. My actions were wrong, and I have come to apologise and make amends. You asked for an explanation, and I am trying to give you an honest one. I cannot pretend my previous actions were honourable, but I would like to make amends through reparations."

Reparations? Elizabeth wondered whether Mr Darcy intended to bring Mr Bingley back into the fold. After all, Mr Darcy apparently made all decisions for the man. She could see that Jane was agitated, since it was rare for her to display her emotions so openly, especially to a gentleman to whom she was not related. Elizabeth resolved to do all she could to manage the rest of their conversation.

She set down her teacup, took her sister's hand, and gave Mr Darcy an imploring look. "I believe you are not quite finished."

"You will not like the rest any better."

"Yet, we insist on hearing it."

Looking uncomfortable, Mr Darcy continued. "As you know, Mr Bingley's wealth comes from trade, and it is only one generation removed. His grandfather was a merchant. His father expanded into sailcloth at the right time, made a great fortune, and wanted Bingley to elevate the family into the landed gentry.

"He has made the attempt by leasing Netherfield. You are a gentleman's daughter, Miss Bennet, and I understand you know all about being the mistress of an estate, so that does you credit. However, your connexions would not help him as would those he could find elsewhere."

Clearly offended, Elizabeth said quietly, "*That* sounds quite mercenary, Mr Darcy."

"I admit it is! There is no use denying it. Matters of fortune and connexion are routinely used in marriage discussions in our class, and it would be disingenuous to pretend otherwise. You would not marry the son of the butcher or baker, regardless of how amiable you found him."

Elizabeth had the good grace to admit the point with a nod of her head, wondering if the gap between a Mr Bingley or Mr Darcy and a Miss Bennet was as large as that between a Miss Bennet and a street urchin. She did not like the answer.

Much to Elizabeth's surprise, Mr Darcy slid his chair forward so he was facing Jane at only slightly above the distance that would bring Uncle Gardiner into the parlour in high dudgeon.

"I am apologising and trying to make amends, Miss Bennet. I am not trying to justify my actions but to explain them. If I thought I was in the right, I would not be here, or at the very least, we would be having a very different conversation."

Jane's expression softened noticeably. "I imagine this is difficult for you."

He shrugged. "Most things that are worth the while are."

"You may as well finish. I imagine the rest is just as unpleasant."

Darcy settled back, apparently trying to get out of arms' reach, frowned ferociously, took a deep breath, and continued.

"The situation of your mother's family, although objectionable, was nothing in comparison to that total want of propriety so frequently, so almost uniformly betrayed by her, by your three younger sisters, and occasionally even by your father."

Elizabeth paled and Jane gasped in shock, less at the sentiments expressed than by having a man completely unconnected to them lay their family faults out for the world to see.

Mr Darcy seemed unable to continue, apparently not believing he could say something so meanly honest, so Elizabeth assisted him.

"It is true, Jane. Mama spent at least an hour at supper boasting about how you would be mistress of Netherfield before Christmas and how you marrying so greatly must throw her other daughters in the way of other rich men. It was..." She continued with a trembling voice. "It was humiliating. To add insult to injury, I tried my best to get her to be silent or at least quieter, since Mr Darcy was hearing every word with his head looking like a tea kettle about to explode."

Elizabeth raised her voice to a falsetto matching Mrs Bennet in her cups. "'What is Mr Darcy to me, pray, that I should be afraid of him? I am sure we owe him no such particular civility as to be obliged to say nothing he may not like to hear'." She looked at Mr Darcy, whose expression was a curious mix of mortification and amusement. "Is that what you meant?"

He nodded.

With trembling hands, Elizabeth reached for the teapot and refilled their cups. "We all know there is much more. To me, it appeared that had my family made an agreement to expose themselves as much as they could during the evening, it would have been impossible for them to play their parts with more spirit or finer success. Would you concur, Mr Darcy?"

"Yes, Miss Elizabeth. It was my conclusion at the time. Add to that the possibility that Bingley could easily be responsible for a widow and four sisters as well as his own likely spinster sister at any moment! The situation seemed untenable."

Elizabeth wanted to scream...or to throw something...or worst of all, agree.

CHAPTER NINE

⸱●——————————●⸱

Reparations

"YOU SHOULD KNOW I AM UNCOMFORTABLE IN UNFAMILIAR society, but Bingley is my friend. I have been helping him for several years, and he has been helping me. I did not want him to have a marriage of unequal affections. It seemed certain that your mother would push you mercilessly into the match, whether you desired it or not." Mr Darcy added quietly, "As I have admitted, I misinterpreted your feelings, Miss Bennet, and I apologise."

Elizabeth realised Mr Darcy had good intentions. He had managed to describe Mrs Bennet's mercenary nature perfectly. Her mother's insistence that she marry Mr Collins proved that handily.

"You may as well finish," she told him. "My behaviour was as bad as the rest of my family. In fact, from the time Colonel Fitzwilliam told me his story until but two minutes ago, I thought I was the primary culprit. I provoked and teased you every time we met for the entire six weeks, and you spent considerably more time around me than the rest of my family combined."

Elizabeth paused and stared at the floor in humiliation.

"Since you are making such pretty apologies, Mr Darcy, I would like to apologise for my part. I took that first slight harder than I let on, mostly because you were echoing what my mother says daily. I spent the entire time doing my best to antagonise you."

She looked directly at him. "That is why I left Kent early —to save you from enduring my company and to prevent me from saying something very unkind, which I assure you, is well within my capabilities.

"That is why I would not ride in your carriage. I presumed Lady Catherine made you offer it out of politeness. It was bad enough when I turned down Mr Collins's proposal. I did not want to start my mother on yet another rampage."

Darcy looked shocked. "You are entirely in error. I can assure you that neither you nor your sister deserved any censure whatsoever. Quite the opposite, in fact! I believe the two of you were the only true ladies between both households. I am not convinced there are any true gentlemen."

Elizabeth laughed at the indirect reference to the Bingley sisters but hardly heard his disclaimer since it was so widely in variance with what she believed. For certain, Jane was a perfect lady, but Elizabeth was not. It was a known fact, as established and immutable as a law of nature.

Much to her surprise, Mr Darcy once again slid the poor abused chair over, but this time facing her instead of Jane.

"Miss Elizabeth, your manners are not only the best in Hertfordshire but quite likely the best of any lady of my acquaintance...ever. If you include the Bingley sisters and Lady Catherine, you have been exposed to a cornucopia of bad manners, intrusiveness, open hostility, and downright rudeness. Yet, you held your head high and maintained your agreeable disposition and courtesy through it all. If you want someone to censure, you can start with me, but I do so wish you would believe that I admire how you conduct yourselves immensely—both of you."

Elizabeth found it hard to accept Mr Darcy would praise their conduct while chastising that of his own party, even his own relation. Elizabeth owned herself to be somewhat high-spirited, but Jane always acted like a lady.

"I hope you can believe me." Mr Darcy looked as though he could elaborate but instead, excused himself and shifted his chair back into its place.

Apparently, he does not hate me, but excepting Jane, he dislikes my family. Elizabeth supposed it was an improvement in his estimation, but she and Jane were still just as single, just as poor, and had just as few prospects as they had that morning.

"I do thank you for explaining it, sir," Jane interjected.

"I am not finished, Miss Bennet. I do truly, with all my heart, offer my profoundest apologies."

"I accept your apology, and I forgive you."

Darcy seemed relieved. "I thank you, madam. Now we must discuss amends."

Elizabeth finally spoke. "Amends, sir? I assumed your apology and explanation were the amends."

"Not amends but a start. Pretty words are a good start, but insufficient. Bingley has not recovered from his time in Hert-fordshire. In fact, he was quite despondent when we last spoke a month ago, so I strongly suspect he is pining for Miss Bennet. If I tell him what I now know, I am certain he would be calling on you within the week and thanking me profusely."

Jane asked, "You say you could easily, but you have not yet done so?"

"I have not. You are the injured party, so I shall follow

your wishes. I could tell him of my mistaken impression and of your presence here in London before the end of the day—or in a week, or a month, or never. That is your choice."

"Is that the only choice?" Elizabeth asked.

"No. There is another I would offer if you are willing to hear it."

"Which is?" Jane asked with marked curiosity.

Darcy chuckled, then gave them a strained smile. "At the risk of emulating your mother, I can throw you in the path of other rich men." He looked surprisingly shy for one who had been discussing such personal matters and asked sheepishly, "May I discuss it rationally, at the risk of being somewhat untoward?"

Jane seemed both surprised and flummoxed, so Elizabeth gently said, "Carry on, Mr Darcy. You made it this far."

"Let us discuss the 'marriage mart' as they call it in society. You are clearly a beautiful woman, and none could argue. You are gently born and bred, and you know all the duties of the mistress of a house. I have seen you and Miss Elizabeth calling on tenants, visiting the poor, and dealing with tradesmen in Meryton. Your mother is loud and shrill, but she does set a good table, and Longbourn seems to be well managed."

Elizabeth wondered if he intended to offer for Jane himself, but she could not believe he would. There was an enormous gap between seeing Jane with less disfavour and seeing her with true admiration.

As though reading Elizabeth's thoughts, Darcy continued. "Have no fear that I am after you myself, Miss Bennet. I shall admit I like you, but I do not love you, and I fear I shall insist on a love match when I marry."

Elizabeth had to admit sheepishly that she admired him for

his honesty. It could not have been easy for such an obviously private man to make such admissions to acquaintances he did not know well, in the middle of a fraught conversation. Of course, the middle of an intense conversation was probably the only place where he could be so explicit.

Jane released a great sigh. "Lizzy and I swore similar vows. We swore only to marry for the deepest love, although the chances of either of us succeeding are dramatically lower than yours."

Darcy nodded. "That is where I may be able to help you. Think about the things that caused me to dissuade Bingley. You have indecorous relations, weak connexions, and little dowry."

Elizabeth wanted to take offence but had to admit he was correct.

"Suppose I introduced you to society as a family friend, and you do your courting in London? All those problems just…disappear," he said with a vague waving motion of his hands. "You would be connected to the Darcys and the Earl of Matlock. Your less decorous relations would be hours away, not to be introduced before a formal alliance was near. You are a kind, handsome lady of elegance and taste, Miss Bennet. I doubt you would last a Season."

Jane sat quietly, closing her eyes as she mulled his offer. After a moment, she blinked, and clearly still in shock, asked, "Are you offering this, Mr Darcy?"

"I am. I am not only offering, I am *begging* you to accept," he said in a tone of strong conviction.

"But why?"

"The fault is mine and so must the remedy be."

"You take too much upon yourself, sir."

"Miss Bennet, a gentleman always endeavours to correct

his mistakes. This is not only my obligation, but dare I say, it would be my pleasure. My parents would be *ashamed* of my recent behaviour. Now I have a chance to make them *proud*. Why would I reject the opportunity?"

"How would you accomplish such a thing?" Elizabeth asked. "Society would not accept the connexion and would assume you were launching your mistress. Done wrong, it could do more harm than good."

Jane cringed at the suggestion, but Darcy appeared impressed that Elizabeth both understood how society worked and was unwilling to pretend maidenly innocence.

"We could assert a distant familial relationship, or if you are willing to wait, I could introduce you to my sister. If you two became particular friends, which is not an unnatural surmise, it would be usual for her to have you as a houseguest. From there, the possibilities are endless. I could also apply to my aunt for assistance. We could easily add to your wardrobe without breaking propriety by having you share Georgiana's. You are of similar size and colouring. It could all be done with nobody the wiser."

Elizabeth said, "You cannot use Jane's distress to flaunt your wealth, Mr Darcy. There are limits."

"Forgive me. I spoke poorly. Do not suppose I am being altruistic. I believe having my sister spend time with the two of you would be to her advantage. Georgiana was always somewhat shy, but last summer's misadventure has made her cripplingly so. I believe the friendship of two such kind, lively ladies could help her. That is worth a great deal to me."

Jane sat in deep thought for a moment. "So, I have the choice. Mr Bingley remains the most amiable man of my acquaintance and the first truly to touch my heart. He broke it as well, but it is mending slowly. I could, by your calculations, have him back and continue as planned with little effort or risk, or I could enter the arena and try for someone better."

Darcy smiled. "That is the gist of it. I know Bingley to be a good man with no bad tendencies, aside from his lack of resolution and two nasty sisters. I believe the right wife would gently correct both of those faults. I would have no qualms leaving you in his care, and he in yours.

"My only correction is about what you said—about attracting someone better. Society is a double-edged sword. You will attract more than your share of rakes and fortune-hunters. It will require the efforts of my cousin, Lady Matlock, and myself to ensure your protection. You can easily find a more consequential or more learned man than Bingley. Whether you find a *better* man is certainly not guaranteed."

Jane blushed. "I thank you for your generous offer. I suppose I need to choose?"

"Yes, although they are not necessarily exclusive, and you need not decide anything now. If you go into society, you will meet Bingley sooner or later. In fact," he said, giving Elizabeth an amused look, "if you want him, making him earn his way back into your good graces might build his character."

Elizabeth laughed at that, and for the first time, thought it might have been possible to be friends with Mr Darcy, had they started on a better footing.

Jane smiled slyly. "I believe I have had an epiphany. In fact, I believe I can explain everything. Would you object if I answer your question with another question?"

He laughed. "For you, yes. For your sister, I would not be so sure. Miss Elizabeth is far more intelligent than I, no offence intended."

Jane grew serious. "Is there *anything* that Mr Bingley or any of your most trusted friends or relations could possibly say that would dissuade you from the other half of this conversation?"

"Not on your life, Miss Bennet. I am fixed on my course," Darcy said instantly.

Jane graced him with the kind of smile she reserved for someone she truly esteemed. "There is your answer, sir."

"Indeed, Miss Bennet. I understand."

Elizabeth looked between them, puzzled by both their conversation and the odd intimacy of it. "Other half? What other half?"

Jane only smiled at her before turning to Mr Darcy. "You have my answer, sir. You may proceed."

CHAPTER TEN

The Second Half

ELIZABETH LOOKED BETWEEN THEM IN CONFUSION, AND IT GOT worse when Mr Darcy leant closer. It occurred to her that she should feel either offended or intimidated by his action, but all fear had been leached from her for the moment.

"Your sister has divined my intent, Miss Elizabeth. The second half of the conversation is for you alone," Mr Darcy said gently.

"What are you about, sir? We have both already apologised for every offence I can think of. I believe we are finished."

"Not quite. I have things to discuss with you as well. Have I your leave to proceed?"

"You need permission from someone besides Jane?" she asked in exasperation.

He smiled and nodded. He started to speak but seemed uncertain how to begin.

She could not help being amused by Mr Darcy's hesitation. "I see you are having trouble getting started with whatever topic is to be devoted to me. Despite my supposed intelligence, I have no idea what Jane decided. Can you at least answer that?"

Mr Darcy remained tongue-tied.

Jane forestalled him, speaking softly but resolutely. "Lizzy, listen carefully. Set aside any lingering prejudice you may have against Mr Darcy. Will you do that for me?"

When Elizabeth's gaze returned to Mr Darcy, she saw a look that seemed somewhere between nervousness and terror on the man's countenance. She realised it must have taken a Herculean effort for him to come to Cheapside, admit his mistakes, and apologise. She wondered what more he could possibly wish to say.

Jane's voice interrupted her thoughts. "Whatever Mr Darcy or Miss Bingley's interference may have been, it was *Mr Bingley* who decided to abandon me. *He* is the one who spent hours in my company, and *he* was the one who should have known my heart. *Mr Bingley* is the one who could not stop his sisters from insulting guests in his own house. *He* is the one who assigned the job of taking leave to his shrewish sister. Need I continue?"

Elizabeth shook her head. "I understand. Mr Bingley's actions have been feckless, the behaviour of a boy, rather than the man you thought you admired. Mr Darcy must have something difficult to say to me, and you were alluding to the fact that he is not shying away from the challenge. Regardless of the outcome of our conversation, at least he is behaving as a gentleman should. I cannot imagine Mr Darcy has anything noticeably worse to say than we have already heard, but I shall listen carefully."

"Without prejudice?" Jane asked, giving her sister a hard look.

Although she remained reluctant to allow Mr Darcy to

begin their acquaintance anew, Elizabeth agreed. She had already forgiven him his actions but was ill-prepared to trust him completely. Both Jane and Mr Darcy waited for her answer.

"Yes. I shall discard my prejudice to the best of my ability."

Darcy was at a loss, cursing his inarticulateness. At length, he began. "In vain I have struggled. It will not do."

As he drew a breath to continue, he was surprised to find that Miss Bennet had taken hold of his arm. It was a sisterly gesture, entirely devoid of anything improper, but it stopped him short.

"Mr Darcy, you are about to do me a great service. May I repay you in advance?"

He was a bit frustrated at her assumption that he could not speak his own mind, but her look of concern made him wonder if he were about to make a complete hash of things.

After another moment's thought, he finally said, "I would appreciate it, madam. I suspect you have correctly identified my difficulty."

She smiled. "I have, sir. Allow me to save you from yourself...just this once."

Jane turned to her sister. "I desire that for a moment, you look at this from a scientific standpoint, Lizzy. For the past few days, we have been examining the 'Mr Darcy-hates-Elizabeth Bennet' theory, and I believe that it is almost correct. It only lacks refinement."

Hate her? How could she ever believe such a thing?

Darcy's jaw dropped. He stared at Elizabeth, who looked as surprised as he by her sister's words. He had tried to show his feelings in word and deed over the previous hour. He hoped it was obvious he could not hate her, had never hated her.

Miss Bennet continued. "The theory was very close to the truth. In fact, I would hazard to guess that it is only off by one word." She pivoted her gaze to the gentleman. "Am I correct, Mr Darcy?"

"You are," he said, with as much aplomb as he could manage.

"I confess I cannot think of any word I could change to make it fit the facts any better."

As she finished speaking, Miss Bennet moved closer to Elizabeth, took both of her hands, and whispered loudly enough for Darcy to hear. "Change hates to loves and see if it makes sense. Do not evaluate the merits of the assertion. Just see whether it makes sense and fits our observations."

Darcy watched as every manner of expression from incredulity to confusion to anger flickered across Elizabeth's face.

Not only has she no idea of my feelings, she does not seem to welcome them.

Unsure of any words he could say, and certain it was unwise to speak in any case, he acknowledged that his fate was as much in Miss Bennet's hands as hers had been in his. Fortunately, hers were far better hands.

Elizabeth tried to speak several times, but she seemed to be as tongue-tied as Darcy had been. He wondered how many years it might be before they could converse without her sister's help.

Finally, she grew still, and Darcy watched Elizabeth close her eyes as though in deep thought. He had the advantage of having had more than four months to resolve his feelings. She had been afforded less than five minutes. He was a patient man and would give her the time she needed.

After some moments that seemed like forever, she finally said, "Is it true?"

He smiled and leant towards her, making every attempt to look attentive and not threatening. "It is."

Elizabeth looked sceptical. "Those walks at Rosings?"

He winced. "You told me that path was a favourite. I-I suppose you thought you were warning me off, but at the time, I thought you were inviting me."

"You thought I *liked* you?"

Embarrassed, he stared at his hands, then finally looked back at her. "Do you prefer the pretty truth or the real truth?"

"Unvarnished, if you please. I cannot fathom the idea, and I cannot imagine reciprocating, but I do want to start with the truth."

Much as he admired her spirit, Darcy flinched at her resolute words. "I fear it will give you an unfavourable sketch of my character, but I would hope that you will conclude that it is not beyond amendment."

"Is amendment your goal, or is it something you feel you must emulate for a time to accomplish some other objective?"

"It is my goal," he said earnestly, "and I hope you will understand *why* after we are finished."

"You must say it plainly, Mr Darcy," said Miss Bennet, "and you need to hear it without prejudice, Lizzy. You need not accept it as truth, but at least hear what the man has to say."

Swallowing, Darcy began again. "You must allow me to tell you how ardently I admire and love you. I had intended to ask for your hand in marriage before your conversation with my cousin. I now suspect it would have gone badly."

Elizabeth appeared completely astonished by the assertion. "It would have. I would have said—" She stared intensely at her hands for a moment. "Well, it is probably best to forget that. The first time I rejected a proposal of marriage, my suitor would not take 'no' for an answer, so I have resolved to be more forceful in any future ones."

Darcy chuckled and tried to match her impertinence. "Elizabeth, it is my hope that you only have one more proposal and no more rejections."

"Perhaps. Are you planning to throw me in the paths of other rich men?"

The jest could have gone badly, but Darcy met the challenge. "Why would I do that when I have Jane to do it for me?"

Darcy's unconscious use of Miss Bennet's given name, moments after addressing Elizabeth with hers, did not go unnoticed. He reddened. It was a sort of intimacy he had not earned, and he was grateful neither sister felt a need to take him to task.

Having said his piece much faster and with less anticipation than he had planned, Darcy was left wondering if he had advanced his suit or killed it.

CHAPTER ELEVEN

The Third Half

DESPITE HER ASTONISHMENT AT MR DARCY'S SENTIMENTS AND his intended proposal, Elizabeth had, much to her surprise, enjoyed her banter with him. She wondered about the next step. The declaration, coming from a man she thought detested her, had been completely unexpected.

Jane, ever perceptive to her sister's moods, said gently, "Perhaps, Mr Darcy, you might answer a few simple questions." She looked at Elizabeth for permission, and her sister indicated her agreement. "Let us start with the obvious. When? How?"

Mr Darcy furrowed his brow. "Perhaps I can start with when?"

Elizabeth nodded.

"I cannot fix on the hour, or the spot, or the look, or the words, which laid the foundation. I was in the middle before I knew that I had begun. The things I said in the first few weeks are painful to remember," Darcy said in a rueful voice. "I freely admit I was an arrogant, insufferable prig. I am trying to reform my character, to act better. My progress is uneven but measurable."

"I feel no need to relive any pain of those first weeks," Elizabeth said. "You have proved yourself reformed, so may we just leave it aside to be discussed later or never?"

Her words clearly not only surprised Mr Darcy, but they seemed to give him some relief with the implied promise of *later*.

He offered a fond smile before continuing. "I agree. I see little profit in recriminations. After that assembly, we were in company often enough that I first started listening to your conversations, then engaging in them. Your visit to Netherfield to care for your sister helped me along considerably. Perhaps I felt a stab of jealousy when I saw you smiling at Wickham, and I must admit the feeling was foreign to me. By the time of the ball, I was feeling quite enamoured, but in my pride, I still thought you unsuitable with regard to fortune and connexions."

Elizabeth grimaced, but since he had said nothing she did not already know, or in fact, anything with which she particularly disagreed, she did not argue. The fact of the matter was that she was unsuitable for a man of his position. Mr Darcy could do so much better, but since he had not with a decade of effort, she was willing to accept both the censure and the attraction as fact.

"May I ask, what did you think was my reason for asking you to dance at the ball, before our quarrel about Wickham?"

"A bet gone wrong."

He looked a bit startled, as though uncertain if she was being impertinent or serious. "You had no idea of my growing regard last November?"

"I am just barely able to entertain the concept of growing regard *now*! I…" She looked thoughtful for quite some time before continuing. "I just thought of the hackneyed phrase, 'it pains me to say this,' and it surprises me."

He gently whispered, "Why?"

"Because for the first time in our acquaintance, I think it might be true."

She glanced at him to judge his reaction. "I cannot say I *like* you, Mr Darcy, but I do admire the courage and honour you have shown today, and I do not wish to cause you pain. It is ... unexpected."

He grinned. "I shall take what progress I can get, Miss Elizabeth. I consider any reduction in animosity a positive step."

Elizabeth felt the effect of his smile more than she anticipated and far more than she ought. She decided she should put that feeling aside and continue.

"Sir, we have discussed at length my family's improprieties. May we..." She paused, not quite ready to throw his insults back in his face.

Mr Darcy must have noticed her struggle. "I can see your good nature causing you to pause, Elizabeth. Might I address the unspoken?"

Once again, he had used her given name, and once again, he was forgiven for reasons she could not explain. Elizabeth thought it was a far smaller offence than being called 'Miss Eliza' by Miss Bingley, and she had never taken that lady to task. If he was something akin to a suitor, even if her mind could not quite accept the possibility yet, the least she could do was refrain from being stingy with her name.

Jane lent her sister able assistance. "Are you planning to address the hypocrisy of your position, Mr Darcy?"

"Hypocrisy, arrogant presumption, selfish disdain of the feelings of others—there are many names for it. Mrs Bennet is no more loud, shrill, or mercenary than Lady Catherine, yet I dared to criticise your mother. Your youngest sisters are brash and somewhat unruly in their behaviour, but they have not tried to elope with a steward's son, despite my sister's superior education," he said a little morosely.

"Yet," Miss Bennet muttered under her breath.

"I believe we understand, sir," Elizabeth said. "Is part of the character reformation project you are embarked upon turned towards that…inconsistency?"

He leant forward. "It is."

"Then let us leave it in the past and return to the main topic. I think you were beginning to explain why. May I speculate?"

"I would by no means suspend any pleasure of yours," he said with an entirely different expression than the cold reply spoken at the end of the dance at the Netherfield ball.

Elizabeth laughed and presented her theory. "I suspect you enjoyed the fact that my manners always bordered on the uncivil. You were disgusted by the women who always spoke, and looked, and thought for your approbation alone. I roused and interested you because I was so unlike them. Perhaps, in the beginning, you just liked me because I did not like you."

Elizabeth looked somewhat embarrassed by the outburst.

Darcy, on the other hand, was delighted, but as he saw her feelings of levity decrease, he answered in a mood he hoped would meet hers better.

"I suspect you are closer to the truth than you may think,

Miss Elizabeth. After a decade of being chased by the likes of Miss Bingley or worse, you were like a breath of fresh air. I shall not own that I love you now just because you are willing to challenge me, but in the beginning, I believe you have the right of it. That, and the fact that you refused to dance with me —thrice by my count."

Elizabeth stared at the floor and blushed. It was the first time Darcy had seen her embarrassed, and he found her pinked cheeks most becoming.

Miss Bennet took notice as well and said, "That has been quite a number of revelations for one day. Mr Darcy, do you remain steadfast in your ambition?"

"More than ever, Miss Bennet."

She smiled. "You may call me Jane in private since you will be tossing me in the way of rich men soon."

Darcy laughed, happy to have someone with such levity in the conversation, particularly since Miss Bennet—*Jane*—had looked despondent at the beginning. "Pray call me Darcy, as my friends do."

Jane nodded and then turned to look at Elizabeth. "How are you feeling?"

"Shocked, amazed… Confused and a little frightened, I suppose."

"Is there any remaining trace of 'implacably opposed'?"

Unable to look Darcy in the eye, Elizabeth shook her head. "No, it is mostly confusion. I suppose time will tell."

Jane turned to Mr Darcy. "You are an intelligent man. I suppose you know my family has likely not become more decorous in your absence. In fact, with the two of us away, they can only have grown worse."

Darcy leant forward, sliding the chair yet again to get as close as he thought proper—and then six inches more.

"We have only brushed the surface of my hypocrisy, and I would expect we shall plumb its depths. I do not do this lightly. If I have my way, your family will be my relations. They cannot be ignored, but they are an issue for a later day."

He was surprised Elizabeth did not bite his head off at the implication that he thought to do something about them. In truth, he hoped she would eventually welcome his interference.

Boldly, he said, "Elizabeth, pray look at me."

When she slowly raised her eyes to his, he gently said, "I am loath to criticise your family, but let us be honest. They embarrass you as much as me! If we marry, their behaviour will reflect on our family. Their reputations can impact our children. We shall be expected to help them form matches, and it is not an unreasonable expectation, especially after I have done the same for Jane. We—you, Jane, and I—must correct them. The youngest girls are easy targets for rakes and fortune-hunters. We do not need to deal with them now, but it must be done sooner than later."

Rather than protest, Elizabeth simply said, "I agree, and should we come to some sort of understanding, we shall have to deal with my family."

"The situation is not hopeless. We have time, and we have resources. No one in your family is in want of anything save education and discipline. When I consider it, your mother seems more frightened of an uncertain future than mercenary."

'We shall be expected...'
   'We have time and resources...'

Elizabeth realised Darcy was using the word *we* quite a lot. While she thought she probably should protest, she was averse to doing so. Whether that was because she was exhausted or liked the sound of it, she was in no mood to speculate.

"If you will allow one more courtesy, Darcy," said Jane, "repeat after me. Miss Elizabeth Bennet, will you grant me the honour of calling on you with the hope of an eventual engagement?"

Elizabeth glared at her sister, who smiled at her prettily in return. She turned to look at Darcy, who also smiled, his eyebrows raised in amusement.

Wishing happiness did not make him look quite so handsome, Elizabeth took a deep breath and said, "I believe you actually have to say the words, sir."

With a grin that was like the sun rising over Oakham Mount, Darcy dropped to one knee and took her hands before repeating the words exactly as Jane suggested.

Elizabeth looked at him with concern. "You understand this is all very new to me, and I cannot promise success."

"Life never promises success, Elizabeth. The best it has to offer is the opportunity to do our best and hope. That is all I ask."

Elizabeth looked carefully into his eyes and felt something melt inside her. She had no idea whether it was her heart opening to the man before her or just nervousness, but she was willing to find out.

"Yes, I would be honoured to receive your calls and spend time in your company."

Jane and Darcy smiled as though the end of the world had been narrowly averted. Elizabeth smiled in genuine, if bewildered, happiness. If her feelings of elation were not equal to her companions, they were certainly good enough for the moment.

Jane once again took charge in a habit that Elizabeth was not sure she liked. "If you are seeking advice, sir—"

"Always," he replied.

"Perhaps you could call on Lizzy here in town for a few weeks and then proceed to Longbourn. You will have to show you can exist peaceably with our family, but there is no reason to poison the well with too much exposure right away."

Elizabeth laughed. "Jane, that is the most unforgiving speech I ever heard you utter. Good girl!"

Darcy supported the plan and appeared genuinely desirous of getting to know the Gardiners. "Shall I apply to Mr Gardiner for permission to court you or ride to Longbourn?"

The frightened gasp from both sisters answered the last question easily enough.

"Mr Gardiner it is!" he said with a laugh.

CHAPTER TWELVE

Plans and Restrictions

"UNCLE GARDINER, MAY WE SPEAK TO YOU?"

The gentleman looked up from his letter. "Of course, Lizzy. You are looking well enough," he said wryly before turning his attention to Darcy. "And you, sir, are still standing, which is better than I expected."

They stepped inside the doorway and sat down. Jane remained in the hall and pulled the door closed.

Both members of the barely acknowledged couple chuckled nervously. According to the rules of propriety, the past hour's conversation should not have happened. Absent Jane's uncharacteristic fierceness, he and Elizabeth would still be at an impasse and stumbling over words. When Elizabeth spoke first, Darcy felt a surge of affection for how well they had adjusted to such unconventional behaviour.

"Uncle, Mr Darcy has asked to call on me in hope of applying for my hand in the future."

Mr Gardiner looked at Darcy intently, although whether he was studying the man or simply trying to unnerve him was unclear. "Well, this is unexpected. And your suitor's request has been ..." He looked pointedly at Elizabeth.

She blushed. "Accepted."

Mr Gardiner cleared his throat and gave Darcy a stern look. "I suppose we can dispense with the first half of the usual discussion. You wish to marry my niece. You can obviously afford a wife, the settlement will be generous, your homes adequate, and so forth?"

"Yes, sir."

"Not to put too fine a point on it, but you are a man from a social class that habitually exhibits a certain... laxness with regards to gentlemanly behaviour..." He let the sentence trail off either suggestively or menacingly.

"I can assure you, Mr Gardiner, I respect Miss Elizabeth. I shall uphold all vows with honour. I have never indulged in the behaviours you alluded to and never will."

"You plan to marry a woman. She is not a child. While it is true that Mrs Bennet may not understand much of the world, Mrs Gardiner does, and you can be assured that Jane and Elizabeth have been properly educated for whatever they may face in the country or in town."

"I admire that, sir. I hope my wife will do the same for my daughters. I find—" Once again, he believed he had overstepped.

Elizabeth reached over to grip his forearm. There were several layers of clothing between her hand and his arm, but it was the closest contact they had ever had outside of a dance, and the very first time she had ever voluntarily touched him.

"Mr Darcy has, within the last year, learnt a hard lesson about the folly of keeping young girls ignorant of the world. I think we may depend on his good sense to know what to share."

That Elizabeth Bennet had just praised his good sense was an abrupt change. Darcy thought she probably still disliked him somewhat, but he believed this could be the beginning of respect, which he craved just as much as her love.

They were both gloveless, and he did not have the nerve to take her hand, but he did manage to put his hand on her arm. It was awkward but still a thrill to see she did not flinch, and her uncle did not chastise him.

"I have never kept a mistress or visited the bawdy houses, nor will I. I have always known I would have only one woman in my life. It is not a burden for me to make this promise, Elizabeth. True love does not require anyone else." He spoke to Elizabeth, but his words were meant for her uncle as well.

He turned back to Mr Gardiner. "As to gambling, I never wager more than what is in my pocket. I rarely overindulge in spirits and could modify that to never if my cousin did not visit."

Elizabeth laughed at the description. "I can easily imagine Colonel Fitzwilliam in such a state but not you."

"My sister will be happy to give you a first-hand account of our entry into Darcy House the day you refused my carriage."

Mr Gardiner snapped to attention. "Refused his carriage! Did you leave something out of your account, Lizzy?"

Elizabeth looked slightly embarrassed. "I may not have been comprehensive."

"You will be now, if you please."

With that, Elizabeth related her revelatory conversation with the colonel, her request to Lady Catherine for a maid, and her subsequent exit from Hunsford.

Darcy started rubbing circles on her arm as she became slightly agitated in the retelling.

If Mr Gardiner noticed, he chose to ignore it. "I shall take you at your word as to your estimable qualities, sir. Now,

Lizzy, are you entering this alliance with an open mind and of your own free will, or was it because Jane browbeat you?"

Darcy was surprised to find Elizabeth's hand still on his forearm and even more surprised that she gave it a surreptitious squeeze. He thought there was little chance her uncle did not see it, but since the man seemed able to ignore the impropriety, Darcy did not acknowledge the effort.

Elizabeth chuckled quietly. "Jane has grown considerably more forceful in voicing her opinions of late, and she did help me to understand fully what was being offered, but in the end, I know it is my *choice,* and I freely and openly accept Mr Darcy's attentions. He accepts my scepticism. Neither of us is perfect. We each have made mistakes in behaviour and understanding. I cannot say whether this courtship will be successful, but I wish to try my best with an open mind and heart."

"That is all I could have asked or hoped for, Elizabeth," Darcy said quite tenderly.

"Well then, we seem to agree," Mr Gardiner said. "Is there anything else I should know?"

Darcy thought a moment. "I would like my sister to become acquainted with your family, sir."

"Of course! She cannot possibly be any worse than Lizzy's sisters," Mr Gardiner said with a laugh.

"Before I introduce Georgiana, I should like to acquaint you and Mrs Gardiner with her history."

Elizabeth gasped. "That is unnecessary."

Darcy gave her a tender look. "Elizabeth, I wish to make you my wife. Unless I am mistaken, the Gardiners are your closest and most trusted confidants, aside from Jane. That means they will be my closest confidants for many years and Georgiana's as well. It is best to get it out in the open. Believe me that we shall be very judicious about who knows Georgiana's story, but I believe we must trust your aunt and uncle. I have no qualms."

"You have not even met my aunt."

"*You* have, and your trust in her is all I require."

Gardiner interrupted. "From what you have said, I imagine you will tell me something disagreeable about your sister. Let us get to the substance of the problem. Did Miss Darcy do something dishonourable or foolish?"

Darcy grimaced. "The latter."

"And may I conclude from your earlier comments that you would prefer the young lady to be less foolish?"

"Yes, sir."

"Well then, I shall give you a choice—well, actually, no—I shall give your *sister* a choice. Since she did nothing dishonourable, she is welcome in our home and in company with our children.

"You, sir, are prohibited from being explicit about what happened to her. What is done cannot be undone, and we shall treat your sister based on the actions we have seen with our own eyes. Your sole responsibility is to tell Miss Darcy that if she ever wants to discuss anything, she may do so with Mrs Gardiner, Jane, or Lizzy, free of censure—with or without your presence at her discretion."

At Darcy's look of amazement, Mr Gardiner continued. "Do not look so surprised. I strongly doubt that you were the first young man in history to arrive at adulthood without doing several dozen incredibly stupid things. Allow your sister the same latitude."

"I wish it were only dozens," Darcy said, chuckling.

Mr Gardiner laughed with him, "I was hoping you had bested me, but it would appear not."

Elizabeth quite enjoyed the conversation between the two men. She hoped her uncle saw that even if she was not yet a woman in love, she had affection for Darcy—and for good reason. She reflected that either her suitor genuinely respected her uncle after a short acquaintance, or he at least recognised that showing respect to her favourite relatives was a good strategy. Even the latter, she reflected, would be in his favour, although it sounded somewhat manipulative. She had no doubt Mr Darcy, given half a chance, would love the Gardiners as much as she did, and he was obviously willing to do so. That willingness would go a long way.

"Shall we discuss conditions and conduct?" Mr Gardiner asked.

"Uncle, you need have no concerns over our conduct." She removed her arm from Darcy's, ignoring her uncle's eye-roll.

"Do not fret, Miss Elizabeth. Such a discussion is perfectly customary. I would be disappointed if your uncle said anything else."

"Have I any say in these conditions? As you know, I do not care to be managed." Elizabeth turned and made sure Darcy could see as well as hear her intended levity.

"Of course," he said in a relieved voice. "You have the ultimate say on the outcome of this endeavour, so agreeing to an alliance when you object to the conditions would be ridiculous."

She nodded in agreement, and then they both turned their attention back to her uncle.

Mr Gardiner looked serious. "Given the contentiousness of your path to this point, I suggest you call on my niece for two months, here and at Longbourn, with no wild plans to propose marriage in a moment of weakness a week or two into your courtship."

Elizabeth, still at the stage where two years seemed insufficient to make up her mind, readily agreed.

"A month in London and another in Meryton," said Mr Darcy. "Your niece and I had the same thought."

"Indeed. The Bennets will be your family if this suit goes forward, and you will have to learn to deal with them. Having said that, too much of my sister this early in the game might —" Mr Gardiner paused and threw up his hands.

Elizabeth giggled at how closely her uncle's sentiments mirrored Jane's and finished his thought. "Might starve a slight, thin sort of inclination entirely away as easily as one good sonnet."

Darcy burst out laughing, while her uncle looked on in bemusement.

Taking pity on her relation, Elizabeth explained the joke while reflecting that most of her previous interactions with the man who was courting her ever so prettily had been what she thought of as arguments, but he probably saw as debates.

She reflected that if she adjusted her behaviour to be more proper according to the myriad rules of decorum, she might well starve away whatever they had. If the gentleman fell in love with an argumentative, impertinent woman who held her own in a debate, changing herself into a demure one might convince him that the woman he fell in love with was dead.

It was something worth thinking about, and worth discussing—or more likely—something worth debating.

Mr Gardiner continued. "For the first fortnight, I would like things to be quiet. No theatre visits, operas, concerts, museums, and so forth. Visit here and walk in the park—the usual sort of things. I would rather not have such a fragile alliance appear in the papers before necessary."

Elizabeth had never thought through all the ramifications of a future with Mr Darcy. She would be gossiped about all over town. Her name would appear in the tittle-tattle section of the papers. Her family would be scrutinised. She would have to deal with all the ton's disappointed debutantes and mothers.

Suddenly Mr Darcy's voice was in her ear. "Breathe, Elizabeth," he said with surprising gentleness as he finally took her hand, squeezing it as she looked at him in near panic.

"Yes, you will be in the first circles, and yes, you will face some difficult times, but you survived Miss Bingley's barbs with nary a scratch. The rest are no worse."

Elizabeth smiled at their shared recognition of the lady. "I think not. She only seeks status. Others are already where Miss Bingley only dares to dream."

"Look at me, Elizabeth. I know the *ton*. I have been in the middle of it for a decade. I could not protect a lesser woman, but I can protect you."

"How?"

"Your natural charm will allay most situations with no intervention. I only need to deal with the more stubborn people, which I can and will—forcefully. All will be well."

Mr Gardiner said, "Lizzy, through my business dealings, I have been around the *ton* longer than your paramour, and I believe he has the right of it. Do you trust me?"

"Of course, Uncle."

"Then do! Your Mr Darcy's mettle is up to the task. Had he come up short, we would be having a very different conversation."

Elizabeth relaxed slightly. "How many other surprises await me?"

"Well, the paths around Pemberley are so extensive I doubt you will manage to keep your petticoats only *six inches* deep in mud. I would expect a foot at the very least?"

Elizabeth laughed and finally relaxed into the feeling that she just might be onto something good, after all.

CHAPTER THIRTEEN

·•·———————·•·

Rocinante and Sancho

"FITZWILLIAM, IS THAT A HORSE OR A DONKEY?"

The innocent-sounding question, proffered on the lane next to the park the following day, caused different but generally positive reactions among the listeners.

Elizabeth could see Darcy was pleased she was not only openly using his given name but teasing him in a manner much closer to her natural disposition. She hoped he did not notice she delivered it with a nervous smile.

Her jest was only another attempt to make him less intimidating. He was doing a good job of that himself, arriving at Gracechurch Street on a nondescript mare rather than his usual fine stallion. He dressed much more like Mr Gardiner than Mr Darcy, and she wondered whether he had sent footpads to steal his clothes from a minor country squire.

Her small cousins, Miles, Juliana, and Silas Gardiner, giggled. "It is a very fine-looking donkey, Mr Darcy," cried Silas, the eldest at six years old.

Darcy dismounted gracefully, bowed to Elizabeth and Jane, and confirmed Silas's opinion. "Rocinante is either a spavined nag or a mighty steed appropriate for a quest."

Elizabeth laughed heartily in great surprise and genuine mirth. "Are we to be tilting at windmills today?"

"Of course, Dulcinea," he said with an exaggerated bow, even lower than Mr Collins, which set everyone laughing.

Darcy offered less ridiculous bows to the company while Jane provided introductions to the children, who bowed and curtseyed with varying levels of success. Elizabeth was surprised that the young children were not intimidated by the tall gentleman, but then reasoned that to a small child, the relative size difference between Elizabeth, Mr Darcy, and a bear was minor.

Darcy gave a passing boy a few coins to take his horse to the Gardiner stables, then offered his arm to Elizabeth so they could proceed. She took it somewhat nervously. Their previous meetings had taken place within the Gardiners' home, but they were in public. Darcy had spied the ladies walking with the Gardiner children and taken Elizabeth's outburst as an invitation to join them.

"Tilting at windmills?" Jane asked.

"It is from *Don Quixote*. It is generally considered the first modern novel and one of the best ever written. Cervantes was a contemporary of Shakespeare."

Elizabeth liked the way he explained the reference to Jane, simply and without any condescension. It was what she would expect of a well-educated man, but sadly, not what she would get from her father.

Jane had abandoned all efforts to discuss such things with Mr Bennet years earlier, chiefly because she did not have the stomach for the scorn she would get if she had trouble understanding something with less quickness than her younger sister. Elizabeth had been unaware of the practice until recently, and she was still quite angry with her father over it.

She looked up at Darcy. "How did you have confidence I would understand such obscure references?"

He looked somewhat embarrassed. "At Lucas Lodge, the first time I heard you play, I was..."

Elizabeth could see him struggling and finished for him. "Determined not to like me."

"Yes, I suppose it was something like that," Darcy said sheepishly.

Elizabeth smiled and encouraged him gently. "Go on. It will get easier over time, and I dare say I would have an equally hard time speaking of my feelings on that night."

"Yes, but I would like to hear them when you are able."

"You will."

Darcy took a breath to regain his place. "That night was when my fascination began in earnest. In fact, after you played, I rather foolishly put Miss Bingley in her place after some derogatory comment about the company by telling her, 'I have been meditating on the very great pleasure which a pair of fine eyes in the face of a pretty woman can bestow.' Needless to say, she was less than amused to discover to whose face those eyes belonged."

Elizabeth blushed furiously to hear him speak that way in front of Jane and the children, although the little ones were not paying the slightest attention. Of course, admitting he admired her, even a little and against his will, a fortnight after the slight at the assembly did not hurt the man's case. To admire her and still treat her as he had was a definite mark against him, but to be spoken of with genuine, if reluctant, admiration was some-what in his favour.

She saw Jane smile. Although her sister was keeping a careful eye on the children and doing her best to remain invisible—or as invisible as Jane Bennet could be—Elizabeth knew she was listening to their conversation and enjoying it.

"I was fascinated by your conversations. You showed a skill I envied. You could patiently speak to Mrs Long about something you must have already heard hundreds of times or discuss a book with Miss Lucas with the skill of a Cambridge man. You referenced three or four things from the book that night. I can assure you that hearing a discussion about a centuries-old Spanish novel does not happen in London every day."

Elizabeth laughed. "Not in Hertfordshire, either—or even in my company, for that matter. Charlotte had just finished what was reputed to be a good translation that was different from the one I read. I do not believe we discussed it or even thought about it before or after."

Elizabeth found that her hand on his arm, which had started out as tense and tentative, had relaxed as they proceeded along the path.

Jane broke into the conversation. "I imagine I can trust you two as long as you stay on the path. I believe I hear the ducks calling for dried bread. You need not remain in sight, but I would ask you not to wander too far."

When Darcy bowed and Elizabeth nodded in agreement, Jane lifted little Miles to her hip, took Juliana's hand, and set out at speed for the pond, chasing after Silas and laughing.

The couple wandered along the path around the small lake, still well within sight of Jane, who was ostensibly acting as chaperone.

After a few minutes of innocuous conversation, Darcy felt the tension in her arm lessen, while her grip on his elbow paradoxically relaxed and tightened at the same time.

Darcy did not mind Elizabeth's nervousness in the least. She was entitled to it. The fact that on this particular day, she was presently not quite as good at hiding her apprehension as usual was of no matter or perhaps even a good thing. He was certain at other times she would appear impervious while he became a stammering green boy in turn.

He had not liked Elizabeth's characterisation of his behaviour that long-ago night at Lucas Lodge, nor the way she flinched when she said it, but he thought the subtleties of that encounter could wait for a more private discussion—especially since, in essentials, she was correct. What mattered was that her hand was on his arm, and he had made her laugh.

"I hope you do not mind my teasing you in front of the children."

He smiled. "Actually, I am delighted to be teased by you. I suspect about half of your conversation now is carefully thought out with a plan, and half is just blurting out whatever comes to your mind in a blind panic."

Elizabeth looked almost embarrassed. "It is calculated. I accepted your suit with the promise I would give it my best effort. I realise we hardly know each other. I hid much of my character from you—as you, sir, hide much of your character from the whole world, or at least the part of the world with which I am familiar."

"I believe you had the right of it at Rosings. I need to practise. In fact, I find practise is always more effective with instruction so…"

Elizabeth laughed. "You think I am to instruct you?"

"Either that or at least give me someone to practise with."

"Why not your cousin? He seems practised enough," she asked in genuine curiosity.

"We know each other too well. Sadly, we exacerbate each other's worst tendencies and have for many years." Darcy looked at her in earnest. "Colonel Fitzwilliam is not such a gossip any other time. He is a better man than you would believe from your brief acquaintance. Having to tolerate the company of Lady Catherine and me at the same time can prompt him to speak out of turn."

Elizabeth thought for a moment. "That is good to know. To tell the truth, I quite liked the colonel until that last day. You need not worry that I had any aspirations towards him or that he had touched my heart in any way, but I did like him and hope he will not feel any awkwardness."

"He will not if I tell him you have forgiven him."

"Tell him I have forgiven him—so long as he does not bring it up again. I am quite finished with that subject. Well, almost."

Darcy was not certain he liked the sound of that. "Almost?"

Elizabeth shrugged. "Jane's advice about the order of apologies was sound. If there are many things to discuss, sometimes it makes little difference what order they come in, but may I defer that for a few minutes?"

"Of course, Elizabeth. I am happy just to be here. I shall follow your guidance."

"I hope you do not always plan to continue this docility. That would be as disagreeable as the converse."

"I suspect we each are pushing our passivity to its limits. I should estimate that by our wedding day, neither of us will have any left. It will be open warfare for the next fifty years."

Elizabeth did not react to his slightly premature mention of a wedding day. "If you do not mind, I wish to discuss our connexion."

"That is why I am here."

She was silent as though deep in thought. "It seems to me that we are in an unusual position. Neither of us knows the other well. You know the kinds of things about me that you could learn by observation, but you obviously do not know me deeply, if your pride made you think I was waiting for an offer or that I would accept one with no real attempt at wooing. Your initial slight altered my opinion of you so badly that I have looked at every interaction since through a lens of prejudice. We each have our perceptions of one another, but we have hardly any idea about the person beneath."

Darcy tried to show no discomfort at how Elizabeth described their situation, and she went on with her explanation.

"It is not unusual because the rituals of courtship generally prohibit any deep knowledge. We are speaking far more directly than most couples. Jane and Mr Bingley would probably have married without your interference, yet neither of them knew much about the other. I would bet Mr Bingley was unaware of much beyond the fact that Jane is beautiful in the way he prefers and that she is kind and amiable in company.

"Even today, Jane knows little more of Mr Bingley than she did that first night when she said he was just what a young man ought to be—sensible, good-humoured, lively, and with such happy manners."

Elizabeth frowned slightly. "Both of their estimations were based on cursory descriptions of their appearance and manners. I doubt either of them really knew anything about the other in any depth, despite the hours they spent in conversation. If Mr Bingley truly knew my sister, you could not have pried him away."

Darcy finally ventured, "Some might argue there is not much more to know about Bingley, but I believe he does have some hidden depths to plumb. The right wife would be able to do it."

Elizabeth changed course. "Uncle Gardiner is not much younger than my mother. He wished to establish himself in his business before he wed, and my aunt's father encouraged that thinking. Thus, my aunt and uncle courted for two years before they married. That is the reason my cousins are so much younger.

"They are the best matched and most content couple I know. I use that word deliberately. When things are going well, they are the happiest of any couple of my acquaintance. However, when things are difficult, they act upon and surmount the problem together. At that time, even though they may not be happy, they are content in their alliance."

"I admire that. Do you think they would offer advice? It cannot hurt to discuss such things with people who have made a successful marriage."

Elizabeth's countenance showed she wondered if he were sincere. The trust in Darcy's eyes must have convinced her that he was being candid.

"Of course! They are quite happy to dispense advice to me, and I believe they will not be opposed to offering it to you if asked.

"Now, on the other hand, my parents were betrothed within less than a month and married in less than three. Their entire courtship lasted roughly as long as Mr Bingley called on Jane. I think I need not tell you it is a misalliance."

"I would not say it, but I shall listen and agree."

"None of that. I insist that neither of us repress what we think. I suspect it will be far from the worst conversation we ever hold."

Darcy wished he could see that same fire in Elizabeth's eyes from something other than anger. He thought he would enjoy kissing away her fury. "That is as things should be!"

"My aunt and uncle were half in love almost immediately, but Uncle Gardiner planned for the future. He refused to have a wife until he was certain he could support her and their children appropriately. He was thinking about the cost of apprenticeships for his sons and dowries for his daughters before he even proposed to my aunt."

"I admire that. It must have been difficult."

"It was. He is successful now, but he did not start that way," she said in a tone indicating the subject was closed.

Darcy thought a moment, trying to keep pace with a woman who was very quick-witted. "How does that pertain to us, I wonder. Obviously, I can afford a family of any size or composition."

Elizabeth stared at the ground. "I would like to make an agreement with you."

"Of course."

"You do not even know what I shall ask."

"You will not ask for anything I shall not accept."

She frowned and scowled with a level of anger that surprised him, leaving him with no idea what he had said to offend her.

"I could ask for any number of things," Elizabeth said. "You have no idea whether or not I am reasonable. I know you think you love me, and you may even be well on the way to loving the true me and not the imagined woman you have in your head. Until you know me better, you should assume I can be both unpleasant and unreasonable."

She finally whispered, "You *diminish* me by agreeing to something without truly knowing me well enough for the trust to make sense."

Darcy looked away, staring at the park's greenery while he considered her words. Elizabeth wandered idly along beside him, making sure he stayed on the path and did not happen upon others.

"I must admit I thought agreeing in advance was a compliment to you, but I can now see that it was not showing you proper respect," Darcy finally said with a nod. "I assumed you were incapable of envisioning some scheme that was too much for me. It presumes you are powerless."

"Exactly!"

"It is a mistake I shall try not to repeat, since apparently," he chuckled, "I would do so at my peril."

Elizabeth laughed along with him, feeling more optimistic about their match. He had given her the respect of listening to her opinion and believing it. She could count on one hand the number of men she knew who would do so, and it did not require all her fingers. She sometimes thought she might not even need more than her thumb.

She drew a deep breath. "Fitzwilliam, my uncle will not entertain notions of an engagement for at least two months, but I suggest we adjust the timing."

She looked up and saw Darcy was frowning. She shook her head. "I do not mean to lengthen it but to ensure the extent of it. Let us agree to two months to the day—no more. During that time, unless something terrible happens or one of us detects some heretofore hidden character flaw, neither of us can beg off. We shall persevere through thick and thin, anger and ardour.

"During that time, we shall demand of each other absolute and total honesty, as though we were already wed. At the end of two months, we shall either be betrothed or forever parted."

She was breathing fast, more from the distress of speaking so forcefully than from the effort of saying so many words in such a short time. She was almost afraid to see how her suitor was dealing with the first big test of their alliance.

She had drawn to a halt while speaking, being almost oblivious to her surroundings, so she was unsurprised to see his boots stepping in front to face her.

Darcy used the knuckle of his hand to lift her chin gently and look into her eyes. "I very much like your plan, my love. I agree!"

His gentle care for her feelings overrode his faux pas in prematurely calling her 'my love'.

Elizabeth decided they had had enough seriousness for one day. "That went better than expected. Shall we leave off courting and walk for a while?"

"It would be my greatest pleasure."

CHAPTER FOURTEEN

•●————————●•

Every Half an Hour

THE NEXT DAY IN THE GARDINERS' PARLOUR, DARCY SMILED as he completed the introductions between his relations and Elizabeth's, primarily because he knew everyone was determined to please and be pleased as much as possible. It was not strictly a proper introduction, but Elizabeth had suggested during their ramble in the park the previous afternoon that her relatives had a sense of humour, so he introduced his cousin as 'Colonel Lunkhead' to cut the tension.

"Miss Darcy, you are most welcome. Colonel Fitzwilliam, you are as well, I suppose." Mr Gardiner laughed heartily.

He led the young lady to sit between Jane and Mrs Gardiner, who immediately welcomed her visitor.

"Miss Darcy, you look very much like your mother, which can only be considered the greatest compliment. I was raised in Lambton. I was not introduced to Lady Anne, of course, but I saw her in the village from time to time, and she was kind and generous to all."

Georgiana smiled eagerly, and their conversation transitioned to talk about Lambton, common acquaintances, and Mrs Gardiner's recollections of Lady Anne Darcy.

Elizabeth knew Mr Gardiner had been in and out of Lambton for several years and had his own recollections to add, and he would likely speak of them to Mr Darcy when the ladies retired to the drawing room. For the moment, he seemed content to let his wife and niece coddle the youngest Darcy.

Elizabeth happily let her elders carry the conversation, and she was glad to have help bringing out Miss Darcy. She had the look of someone who was naturally shy, but those who could retain their reticence against a sustained assault from Mrs Gardiner and Jane were few and far between. Miss Darcy looked nervous on first sitting down, but within a quarter of an hour, Elizabeth thought she was perfectly relaxed.

While the women talked among themselves, Elizabeth became strongly aware of her suitor, sitting next to her on the sofa. Although Darcy and the colonel gave the bulk of their attention to Miss Darcy's conversation, Elizabeth felt an undefined intensity in sitting so close to her suitor. She could not precisely say whether the feeling was one of attraction or nervousness, but she surmised the two feelings were similar enough to confuse easily.

Elizabeth had chosen her seat carefully before the party entered. It was another deliberate attempt to make the man less of a mystery, to make him less fierce, to force them to interact more and more closely. She was slightly nervous about their two-month agreement, but she was unwilling to change it. On reflection, Elizabeth thought her previous feelings of dislike and disgust towards Darcy were well dead and buried, but she was still uncertain what would replace them.

The prior evening after their walk in the park, Elizabeth had tried, mostly in vain, to fall asleep. As she tossed and turned, she recalled a conversation between herself and Charlotte at Lucas Lodge. Charlotte believed Jane did not exhibit her feelings enough, while Elizabeth contended it was the gentleman's job to discover them.

At the time, she had thought Charlotte either mercenary or practical—almost synonymous in her mind—and history had proved her correct. Eventually, Elizabeth decided Charlotte had made the correct decision for herself, even though it obviously would not have done for Elizabeth. Time would tell if it was a good choice, but Charlotte and Mr Collins appeared content enough. She also concluded that Charlotte had been right about Jane, at least based on Jane's desires at that point. Elizabeth remembered the conversation almost verbatim and lay in her bed recalling the part about affection.

Charlotte had asserted that Jane's sweet placidity did not allow others to see her as a lady of deep feeling. "There are very few of us who have heart enough to be really in love without encouragement. Bingley likes your sister undoubtedly, but he may never do more than like her, if she does not help him on."

"But she does help him on, as much as her nature will allow," Elizabeth had argued.

Charlotte had been unpersuaded. "He cannot know Jane's disposition as you, as her sister, do."

"But if a woman is partial to a man, and does not endeavour to conceal it, he must find it out."

"Perhaps, if they are enough in each other's company. Although Bingley and Jane meet tolerably often, it is nearly always in large mixed parties. Your sister should make the most of every half an hour in which she can command his attention. When Jane is secure of Mr Bingley, there will be more leisure for falling in love as much as she chooses."

Therein lay the problem! How many of Elizabeth's current difficulties would have been avoided if she had just had *one* honest conversation with Mr Darcy? She would have been well within her rights to call him to task as early as the Meryton assembly. She could have let him know about her low opinion when she was staying at Netherfield, but she so enjoyed disliking him, the thought never occurred to her. While it was easy to believe she had simply been as polite as she could around people she disliked, Elizabeth had to admit she went out of her way to punish the man whenever possible. Mr Wickham's lies had found fertile soil, but she had been working that garden for a month before the man appeared.

All those thoughts led Elizabeth's mind to circle around to a completely different one that was startling and kept her awake another hour.

Had she obtained an apology, or not heard the slight in the first place so that she treated him as an indifferent acquaintance, would Darcy have fallen in love with her? Was he in love with the prickly, impertinent Elizabeth Bennet or with the more ordinary incarnation? Would he have simply ignored her and carried on with his life? More to the point, would he maintain his affection when she no longer displayed the sharpness she had shown in Hertfordshire?

In the end, there was one thought that had finally allowed Elizabeth to rest, one thought that put her mind to the place where she could at least sleep and ruminate in peace.

It did not matter!

Charlotte, either through wisdom or sheer luck, had said two things in that pretty little speech that told her how to think and act—and at least to sleep.

"There are very few of us who have heart enough to be really in love without encouragement."

That was an immutable fact that nobody could dispute. It was difficult to fall in love without encouragement, but Darcy had done so. He had, through whatever mysterious process on which his heart and his mind relied, concluded that he loved her, that he wanted her, despite any number of rational objections—and without any encouragement whatsoever.

More importantly, his actions proved beyond any reasonable doubt that the gentleman was willing to fight for her. It could not possibly have been easy to come to Gracechurch Street and face both sisters, yet he had done so. It would have been far easier for him to speak to them one at a time or abandon the project altogether. In the end, he did what was both the right thing and the difficult thing.

That important realisation gave Elizabeth a warm and comfortable feeling. It was the last thought she remembered before falling blessedly asleep, and it was her first thought on waking.

When she heard the Darcy coach on the drive, one more piece of advice from Charlotte had come to mind—that Jane should make the most of every half an hour in which she could command Mr Bingley's attention.

This, Elizabeth realised, could work in reverse. They had sixty days with significant relaxation of the usual rules of propriety to decide whether they suited each other enough to make a lifetime commitment. She did not need to make the most of every half an hour as Charlotte asserted, but at least Elizabeth certainly had to make the most of every day.

With a start, she brought her focus away from her ruminations and remembrances and back to the party in front of her.

With Miss Darcy in good hands, she spoke softly to Mr Darcy. "I am not certain you will ever be able to pry your sister out of this house, and she has not even seen the children yet."

"That statement rests on an invalid assumption, Elizabeth."

The way he said Elizabeth created a bit of unrest in her stomach. It was a sort of…something she could not put a name to, but if someone asserted it was the start of affection or even passion, she could not argue. Elizabeth found the feeling thrilling and frightening in equal measure. It was almost as though he managed to put a caress into merely speaking her name.

She tried to recover her equanimity. "After such a bold statement, I believe you must clarify, sir."

Darcy gave a whimsical smile that she had to admit was quite endearing. "That presumes I want to pry her away. I can just as well return in a month or two. Mrs Gardiner seems as though she could use practise for her girls."

Elizabeth laughed and relaxed slightly. "Since Miss Darcy seems happy enough and the colonel could gossip with a rock, do you suppose we could entice them into the music room, so we can sit and talk? We have things to discuss."

Darcy looked a bit concerned. "I applaud the plan, but Georgiana is shy. I am not certain she can be coerced into playing."

"I see you have not quite learnt that you underestimate Jane and my aunt at your peril. Your sister will play and mine will sing! There can be no two opinions on the subject or any two possible outcomes once they put their minds to it. Her reticence is doomed."

Darcy laughed. "Your sister seems to be more…*resolute* than she was earlier in our acquaintance."

Elizabeth wondered what to say, as she found the cause of the change in Jane to be a mystery. Finally, she said, "Jane's pleasing countenance is the same thing as the fearsome Darcy scowl. It is a mask, and I believe four months of heartache convinced her to give it up, at least sometimes. I shudder to think what will happen the next time my mother starts blath-ering that Jane cannot be so beautiful for nothing. I suspect Mama has a hard lesson coming due."

"I can assure you that being taken to task by your sister builds character, so perhaps your mother will profit from the experience."

Elizabeth grinned, but the thought gave her something to think about later in privacy.

She had, of course, already arranged a plan with Jane, so a nod of her head prompted the rest of the party to rise and move from the parlour to the drawing room. Jane had a lovely singing voice but no skill whatever at the pianoforte. Geor-giana reportedly had skill in abundance but was shy. Jane's task was to get the two of them playing and singing using whatever persuasion was required.

Once everyone was settled to their satisfaction, and one song had been performed and applauded appropriately, Eliza-beth and Darcy began speaking quietly. The others talked softly amongst themselves while Jane and Georgiana spent some time choosing another song and chatting amiably, looking for all the world like the best of friends.

"I am glad our sisters get along so well," she commented.

"As expected," Darcy replied. "My sister would like to be known by her given name. If you simply adopted it without asking, she would enjoy it."

Elizabeth smiled. "Very well, Georgiana it is, or would she prefer something shorter, like Georgie?"

"I suppose a woman with a four-syllable name is quite inclined to shorten all names."

"Yes, but at Netherfield, you could have taken care of Mr Bingley's requirement that you struggle for words of four syllables by simply writing my name several times in your letter to your sister."

Darcy's grin grew practically from ear to ear. "What do you think I was doing?"

Elizabeth gasped. "You were not!"

"Yes, my dear, I believe I was well and truly hooked. Like the trout, I fought the line as long as I could, but I think my fate was sealed even then. I had to defer conveying Miss Bingley's raptures because I was writing about you."

Elizabeth let the use of 'my dear' go by without comment. It seemed to be an ingrained habit with the man, and if they were to make this a successful match, she would not oppose any such endearments. She had become somewhat accustomed to such declarations. However, the rest of what he had said was troubling.

She sighed. "I have difficulty reconciling that time. I had such a low opinion of you that all my memories are tainted and untrustworthy." Elizabeth looked around to ensure they were in private conversation before looking him in the eye and continuing in a soft voice. "That said, we come to the most difficult part of this courtship."

Darcy did not interrupt.

"For certain, there are questions to be raised and answered, but the core truth is that you felt some infatuation, apparently nearly every day for four months. Yet, right up to the day you claim you would have proposed, you still felt me *inferior* in some way. It is difficult to reconcile."

"Do you believe my pig-headedness is likely to be the biggest stumbling block or perhaps, that aspect combined with my less than gentlemanly manners, along with pride not under good regulation?"

Elizabeth thought for some time, finally allowing, "I

thought your manners dreadful, but on reflection, I cannot find true fault, other than at that first assembly, of course. I suspect if I had a full accounting of the discussions held at Netherfield behind my back, I would be less sanguine, but I cannot honestly say that you have been ungentlemanly in my presence."

"You are correct about things I either said behind your back or allowed the Bingley sisters to say without challenge, which is almost as bad." He frowned unhappily. Clearly, he thought it was of utmost importance to accept blame.

Elizabeth did not quite like that. She reached down and briefly squeezed his hand, which was sitting atop his thigh.

"I would beg you to take responsibility for your own actions and yours alone. I shall account for my own. Giving too much weight to those that surround us is how we came to misunderstand each other. I feel no great compulsion to take credit or fault for my mother or younger sisters, nor should you be taking responsibility for two indifferent acquaintances. If the behaviour in the Bingley household was not proper, was it not for the head of the *Bingley* family to set it right?"

Darcy nodded at her reassurance and reached to take her hand back in his. She smiled, not in the least discomposed, and even though it may not have been strictly proper, she accepted his hand and kept hold of it.

Leaning her head towards his, Elizabeth whispered, "I suppose the root of the problem is that we need to spend time together and see whether our feelings match our expectations. I need to see whether I come to love you as you think you love me, and you need to see if you love the real me instead of the pretend me that I have always shown you."

Elizabeth smiled up at him. "I have been thinking about you. In a way, our shared history is our worst defect. In many ways, we should be a very good match, perhaps even exceptional. Your talents and disposition as I see them now seem as though they should be able to answer my own. Perhaps I flatter myself that through my ease and liveliness, your mind might be softened, your manners improved. Conversely, I have lived a sheltered life, and I believe that through your judgment, information, and knowledge of the world, I might receive benefit of great importance. Naturally, your education, your experience, and your situation in life are far superior to mine, but I do not believe I would come into this without value."

Darcy smiled and boldly turned his hand over to interlock their fingers. "For certain, you bring much to this union. In fact, you bring everything that is truly important."

Darcy paused for a moment in apparent deep thought. "Let me ask you something, Elizabeth. Suppose for a moment I wanted a woman with the situation expected of a man in my position—a woman with sufficient beauty, the right accomplishments, appropriate connexions, adequate dowry, a disposition that I could at least live with, healthy enough to give me an heir and a spare—and I was not looking for a love match. How long would that take?"

She gave the question some consideration. "A month, maybe two—at most, a Season. Probably less if you ask one of your aunts to take up the task."

"Yet, ten years on, I am here begging for your hand in Cheapside."

Elizabeth blushed but felt surprisingly happy that he had managed to say that in a way that did not denigrate Cheapside or her family in the least. His tone of voice, now that she understood it, made the admission more like an affectionate joke between friends. He was saying there were treasures to be found in Cheapside that he would have been unaware of, not that it was a location to be disdained as the Bingley sisters had.

She smiled and pressed his hand harder. "Yes! Here you are, and dare I say it," she looked down at their entwined hands, then back to him, "in fifty-eight days, you may not have to beg."

Darcy smiled smugly.

CHAPTER FIFTEEN

The Four Elements

THE FIRST FORTNIGHT OF DARCY'S PURSUIT OF ELIZABETH'S hand had been filled with visits to Gracechurch Street, with or without the colonel and Miss Darcy. He had hoped to host everyone at a dinner at Darcy House, but Elizabeth had been reluctant to consent.

Darcy understood her hesitation. At present, only six trustworthy people knew about the attentions he was paying to her. The notice that would result from such a public declaration of his interest as being seen with him at his home, the theatre, the opera, or any of the other several dozen things he had hoped to do in their month in London was something entirely different. Her name would be bandied about in the tittle-tattle section of the papers, and speculation would run rampant once he showed a clear public preference. Elizabeth insisted she wanted to manage the news about herself in her own time, and he could not argue the point. He was aware she needed to be more certain of her feelings before entering the arena, and he could not blame her in the least—no matter how frustrating he found it.

Darcy called on Elizabeth nearly every day and stayed for

dinner most evenings. Georgiana attended the Gardiner residence at least half a dozen times and seemed content to lock herself in the nursery with the children or in the music room with Miss Bennet, leaving her brother to his own devices. Colonel Fitzwilliam also made frequent appearances, and spent his time with Mr or Mrs Gardiner, depending on who was about.

"Your beau seems confused, Lizzy. He appears to be romancing the entire Gardiner family," her uncle said when he, along with Darcy and the colonel, joined the ladies after spending time together in his study, the door barred against all female incursions. Meantime, the ladies had spent the hour with Jane and Georgiana practising a duet, while Elizabeth and Aunt Gardiner gave lessons to some of the older children.

"Not confused, Uncle. It is strategic! Mr Darcy knows which side his bread is buttered."

Not to be outdone, Georgiana laughingly added, "Yes, and he realises your good opinion is quite difficult to earn."

Darcy smiled at the twin jests, feeling inordinately happy that the mixed company of the Bennets and Gardiners seemed to have given his sister the remedy for her melancholy of the past summer. He laughed with everyone else, then took Elizabeth's hand for a quick kiss. Though it did not make her blush, he felt her shiver.

While Darcy understood he needed the approval of the Gardiners to call on Elizabeth, he liked to think if he met them independently, he would have been fond of them on their own merits. Of course, before he met Elizabeth, it would have been unlikely. Despite her previous assumptions, it was not that he disdained the area in which they lived, he simply had no business there. Any friend of Mr Bingley had no cause to look down his nose at tradesmen. In fact, Darcy anticipated having Mr Gardiner help him with some investments of his own.

The party sat down for the tea that had been used as a lure to rescue the men from each other's company. Darcy sat by Elizabeth, and he noticed the selection of biscuits and sweets were his and Georgiana's favourites. He assumed Elizabeth or Mrs Gardiner did that as a matter of courtesy, not that he was complaining.

After a bit of tea accompanied by a light discussion, he glanced at the colonel. Nodding, Darcy cleared his throat and looked directly at his lady.

"If you have no objections, my cousin and I would like to discuss something of import that affects all of us."

"Of course." Elizabeth looked at him curiously.

"I would like to preface this by saying that I value your opinion immensely. I wish that now and in future we discuss all important matters between us, as your aunt and uncle do. There may be instances where I must make a decision and hold to it, but most of the significant ones should be shared."

A small smile appeared and spread across her face. It might well have been the most romantic words the man had ever spoken, and Elizabeth made sure her expression showed approval, even though she could in no way say what she was thinking in such a public setting.

"That said, Colonel Fitzwilliam and I have taken it upon ourselves to deal with a certain situation that concerns all of us without your involvement. I hope you will not find it officious."

"Does this affect me directly?"

"Not yet," he assured her, "but the possibility exists."

"In that case, you need not ask," Elizabeth said calmly. "I am not yet your wife and have no business intruding on your affairs."

Darcy smiled at her inadvertent 'yet,' but nodded to his cousin. "Richard."

The colonel put on as serious an expression as Elizabeth had ever seen. "Wickham has discovered a hitherto unknown streak of patriotism. He has joined the navy."

Elizabeth appreciated that each man was looking carefully at Georgiana. She had emphasised to Darcy and his cousin that if they wished their ward to act like a grown woman, it was vital they begin treating her like one—or at least, as mature as she was likely to be at sixteen years of age.

"The Royal Navy?" Elizabeth enquired. "This comes as a surprise. I had no idea his patriotism ran that deep."

"Neither did he," Colonel Fitzwilliam said with an impertinent grin.

"I see you are eager to explain, Colonel. Proceed at your leisure," Mr Gardiner suggested.

Instead, it was Darcy who continued. "Since leaving Hertfordshire, I have been feeling guilty that I left that wolf in sheep's clothing to continue his predations without warning. The feelings came to a head about a fortnight before you left Hunsford. I had a—" He stopped, seeming unsure of how to continue.

"You may as well say it," Elizabeth said gently. "I shall not censure you."

Darcy gave her a nervous smile. "I was planning to propose to you. I have spoken of my ungentlemanly feelings in enough depth, but I did have some small concern that

Wickham may have imposed on you, or that you might have been taken in by his tales of woe. He is, as you know, the most gifted liar I have ever met. Richard and I sent an investigator to learn how he behaved."

"I suppose you learnt he behaved abominably?"

"Yes. In my defence, I suppose I could say that with him gone, the second-worst scoundrel in the militia company will simply take his place, but that will not be on my head."

Mr Gardiner asked, "Do you expect that transition to take long, Mr Darcy?"

"About ten minutes," the colonel answered. His eyes, like those of Darcy and Mr Gardiner, drifted to Georgiana, trying to gauge her reaction.

"You need not worry about me. That man can no longer cause me pain. I assume you took safeguards to ensure we never meet him again," Georgiana said with a soft smile, not precisely happy, but not distressed either.

Darcy answered for them both. "We did." Then, he turned back to Elizabeth. "The fact that your mother is determined to throw your sisters in the way of the redcoats frightens me. Most of them do not have two farthings to rub together, and although it pains me to say it, I am not certain I ever heard two words of sense from either of your two youngest siblings."

Elizabeth sighed. "I believe the officers dine much better at the homes of the gentry. A bit of flirting with the sillier daughters of the neighbourhood seems adequate compensation for their meals. As for my sisters, I shall be happy when the militia is gone." Elizabeth wondered whether Lydia may have come closer to ruin than anyone expected.

The colonel continued. "As to Wickham, Darcy and I had hoped service in the militia would give him a chance to reform, but he was just as debauched as ever. He never uses force or violence at least, which makes him a step above the lowest of the low…barely."

Elizabeth looked between Darcy and his cousin. Since Wickham had tried to impose on their ward, Elizabeth assumed they felt joint responsibility.

Colonel Fitzwilliam took up the tale again. "I went to Hertfordshire and was feeling somewhat poetic, so I gave Wickham his choice of the four elements."

Mr Gardiner appeared intrigued. "Well, with the Royal Navy, he obviously chose Water. May we presume the others were even less palatable?"

The colonel nodded grimly. "The navy is an honourable profession, far better than Wickham deserves. His life is no more dangerous than the one I chose voluntarily and honourably in the army. It is, however, an institution that is frequently used as a refuse heap for criminals, and they have well-established procedures for ensuring the men act either honourably or fatally. It is Wickham's very last chance."

Elizabeth saw Darcy watching Georgiana. She knew him well enough now to understand that he regretted having left his sister ignorant of Wickham's character.

Georgiana was hearing this story for the first time and reached for Elizabeth's hand but then surprised everyone by saying, "Let me guess! Air would be the infamously bad air in the hulks that serve as makeshift debtor's prisons."

Jane gasped but Elizabeth smiled, realising the growing maturity in the girl likely to be her sister. *She may be past coddling if her brother can bear it.*

"Good guess, Georgie. Your cousin thought you would not take it so well," Darcy said.

She shrugged indifferently. "What was the option for *Earth*?"

The colonel laughed, clearly pleased to see the improvement in his ward.

In a sober voice, Darcy explained. "My investigators found proof Wickham went beyond his usual predations on the night of the Netherfield ball. He went to town and participated in an attempted burglary of a nobleman. If he was brought up, he would be hanged within a week."

"*Earth*, indeed," murmured Georgiana.

Well-read as she was, the conversation about Wickham's deserved fate left Elizabeth with the realisation that her hitherto confined life in Hertfordshire had left her nearly as naïve as Georgiana. "And *Fire* would be?"

The colonel exchanged an uncomfortable look with Darcy, who nodded in what Elizabeth assumed was permission to explain.

"*Fire* would bring Wickham's chickens home to roost. He owes a great number of debts, many with people who do not believe in debtors' prison but prefer to handle matters privately and definitively. They like to set examples. Once I knew his whereabouts and had secured him, I simply offered to acquaint a few of his creditors with his location and refrain from protecting him."

Jane turned pale. "You say this is worse than hanging."

"Far worse! A hanging is over in less than a minute, and that is all I shall say."

"That is all you *should* say, sir!" Mr Gardiner warned.

"I shall add only that if Wickham ever again sets foot in England more than a quarter-mile away from a navy ship, he will go directly to the gallows. The man had every chance in the world, and we shall see if the navy can fix him."

"I am happy you did not challenge him to a duel," Georgiana said quietly.

The colonel snorted in amusement. "That would just be a less official flavour of *Earth*."

"Well," Mrs Gardiner said in a firm voice signalling the maudlin conversation was at an end, "I believe a small walk might be welcome. Would you take the children to the park for an hour?"

"It will be our privilege," the colonel said, rising quickly and offering his arm to Jane.

Elizabeth looked at the pair and bit back a smile. Colonel Fitzwilliam and Jane were well aware he could not afford her as a wife, but their mutual lack of expectations beyond camaraderie and amusement made them the most pleasant company.

CHAPTER SIXTEEN

The Labours of Hercules

ELIZABETH HAD TO ADMIT FITZWILLIAM DARCY, THE fearsome although admittedly handsome master of Pemberley, carrying little Miles Gardiner on his shoulders, while engaging Silas in a long-winded discussion of the fishing he would enjoy when they visited Pemberley, made a pretty picture. The fact that the Gardiners would be welcome at Pemberley regardless of what happened between her and Darcy was a point very much in his favour. His genuine feelings of affection for the Gardiners were a mark of good sense, and Elizabeth could never love an insensible man.

She wondered if the fact that she had to twist her thoughts almost in circles to maintain any pretence of not falling just the slightest bit in love with the man was an indication that she may have fallen farther than she thought.

Since Darcy remained happily distracted, Elizabeth gazed at him with what she did not realise was the same expression he wore when looking at her in Hertfordshire. She could quite easily imagine substituting their own children for the Gardiners'.

The time was coming when their connexion could no

longer be hidden. If she were completely honest, Elizabeth thought the privacy of the past fortnight had served its purpose. She thought herself well beyond rejecting him—assuming he still had the desire to propose in another six weeks. Elizabeth could not imagine he would not. She could sheepishly admit she trusted Darcy in almost every way. His manners might not always be perfect, but they were as good as her own, and his honour and integrity could never be questioned.

She noticed Jane and Colonel Fitzwilliam seemed to get along well but had no idea if the feelings were familial or romantic. Jane was a grown woman, and she knew what she was about. Elizabeth expected nothing would happen but thought that having the colonel as her elder brother would not be the worst possible outcome.

The hour they allocated for their walk flew by, and almost another hour as well. Elizabeth had no idea whether Jane was procrastinating or simply enjoying herself. For her part, procrastination was definitely the order of the day. The early May sun was pleasant, and the energy of the children indefatigable, at least until the moment they all nearly collapsed in a heap, to be carried home half-asleep by the gentlemen.

Mrs Gardiner had refreshments prepared in the parlour when they returned. After the tired children were sent to the nursery, she allowed her nieces to begin the conversation they had requested.

"Colonel, Georgiana, we need to discuss some things that may not affect you, but Jane and I thought you should be included," Elizabeth began.

Both indicated they would be happy to be of assistance. Elizabeth turned to Darcy and took his hand.

Darcy looked down at their joined hands—hers so small in his own—and prepared himself for something dire.

"Jane and I have some rather disagreeable tasks we would ask you to attend to on our behalf. These are not the Labours of Hercules. Be assured my affection does not depend on their completion, but our comfort does, and we would appreciate them done and out of the way."

Darcy thought he would happily do a dozen or more labours if only to see Elizabeth smile at him one more time as she had just done. His heart was bursting, but he nodded in understanding, waiting for her to enlighten him.

Elizabeth nodded to Jane, who began to speak almost reluctantly. "The Bingleys."

There had been no doubt the subject would come up sooner or later. Darcy was only surprised they had ignored it for a fortnight. On the fourth day of his suit, he and Elizabeth had discussed the events between Bingley and Jane in detail. They concluded Bingley was not irredeemable, but it was not the role of the Bennet sisters to redeem him.

Jane looked at Darcy and continued. "We understand Mr Bingley is one of your dearest friends, and neither Elizabeth nor I wish you to lose that alliance. Despite a lack of resolution, we believe Mr Bingley is a fine boy who may one day be a worthy man. Although I shall no longer consider him, we wish him no harm."

'A fine boy' was a harsh judgment indeed. Darcy saw Georgiana shudder and assumed her thoughts had drifted to Bingley's sisters. She did not know Bingley well, but she knew all she ever wished to know about his sisters.

Jane continued. "I would appreciate it if you had a word with Mr Bingley to prevent future awkwardness if we are in company."

"Tell me what you wish said, and I shall say it, Jane."

Darcy still felt contrition for his previous interference, but recognising Jane would probably be much happier without his friend, he found it difficult to entertain any significant remorse.

"Pray tell him I hold no animosity towards him. You may relate, for his own edification, that I suffered heartache for several months if you must, but there is no need. It would probably help build character, but that is not our task. It should have been his father's."

Darcy reflected a moment before replying. "If you truly have no objections, I believe it would be useful for him to know. A man should pay some penance for harming a lady's heart, even if it was inadvertent and you hold no animosity. If he has any scruples at all, he should be made aware that his actions have consequences."

Jane spoke again in a firmer voice. "You may tell him or not, as you choose, but there is one thing I insist upon. Make it known to him that we are now indifferent acquaintances. I shall be polite but distant with him, and I expect the same courtesy. I shall not dance with him, so he should not ask. I shall not cut him, but I shall not give him more than a minute of polite conversation."

"That seems fair. I shall see to it," Darcy said with genuine sadness.

Elizabeth was happy to have that disagreeable task over—or at least in Darcy's capable hands. It would be awkward for him, but he would survive.

"Now we come to the disagreeable topic of sisters," said Jane. "Not my own, but Mr Bingley's."

She reached out to Georgiana and gave her the letter Miss Bingley wrote to her when the party quit Netherfield.

The colonel peered over Georgiana's shoulder to read with her. Elizabeth watched their progress until they reached the relevant part, whereupon Georgiana gasped. "Why, that wicked woman!"

"Is she mad?" the colonel growled. "This is the sort of thing that reputations are lost over. I ought to—"

Elizabeth decided to intervene. "Richard, whatever you have in mind to do, pray do not."

It was the first time she had ever used his given name. She could see his blood boiling, and considering the treatment Mr Wickham eventually got at his hands, Elizabeth thought it best to keep his temper in check before Caroline Bingley joined the navy as well.

"We wanted you to understand, but we have our own request and hope you will heed it," Elizabeth said forcefully.

Much to her surprise, the colonel abandoned the topic entirely and looked at Darcy with a grin. "Ah, the mistress of Pemberley voice. I can hear Lady Anne."

Elizabeth frowned but did not back down.

He chuckled and raised his hands. "Peace, Elizabeth!"

Darcy cleared his throat. "Jane, pray continue."

"I would wish one of you to have a direct conversation with the, um…lady?"

Phrasing it as a question left Georgiana giggling in an entirely too Lydia-like manner. Elizabeth laughed properly, and even Jane smiled at her own jest, even though it had been accidental.

"Tell her that she is unknown to us. If she speaks to any Bennet, we shall give her the cut direct. We shall not go out of our way to break with her publicly, so long as she ignores us." Jane concluded her speech and looked at Elizabeth.

The colonel grunted. "That may be good enough for you but not for me. I have a more vindictive streak. Miss Bingley must curb her gossiping tongue. She must understand any gossip that includes the names Darcy or Bennet that can be traced to her will be treated as a hostile act by my mother."

"You plan to tell her this yourself," Darcy said.

"Of course. In Bingley's presence! It is time for them to understand the precariousness of their position in society. Miss Bingley's mission in life is to climb the social ladder. I can easily chop the legs right off. She needs to understand her own insignificance."

Darcy agreed but thought he would prefer a more diplomatic approach.

Jane sat back, looking relieved and triumphant. "Very well then, I am done thinking about the Bingleys, and I suggest that once you gentlemen have had your conversations, you be done as well."

Mrs Gardiner laughed. "That was easy!"

Darcy, feeling somewhat playful, turned to Elizabeth. "What next, my love? We are less than a fortnight from battling Mrs Bennet and at least ten labours short."

It was a perilous statement, but Elizabeth just shook her finger light-heartedly. His habit of slipping endearments into conversation no longer shocked her. To be truthful, she quite enjoyed it. She supposed that told her something about her feelings. She had to continuously remind herself that his thoughts had been building for months, while her knowledge of them and their alliance had scarcely a fortnight's duration. His willingness to poke fun at Mrs Bennet was also in his favour.

She smiled and swatted his hand playfully. "I know you will find Mama challenging. To be honest, Jane and I find her challenging as well. As you know, I have already written to my father, and we shall return to Hertfordshire in a fortnight as agreed.

"Instead of throwing you directly from the pan into the fire, I thought we should work our way one step at a time, as you might with sport."

Darcy raised an eyebrow to encourage her to continue.

Elizabeth took a shuddering breath. "Before Hertfordshire, we must go to Rosings and inform Lady Catherine and Miss de Bourgh about our alliance. It would be helpful if Richard and Georgiana accompanied us."

Murmurs could be heard between the Gardiners and a gasp from Georgiana.

"Pray explain," Darcy asked cautiously.

"Fitzwilliam, you do not have such a surfeit of family that you would wish to discard them. Right or wrong, Lady Catherine is your aunt, and she does have expectations. If she learns about our understanding from anything other than our own lips, she will be incensed. She will feel betrayed."

Darcy practically snarled. "She can feel as betrayed as she wants. I am not bound to Anne in any—"

Elizabeth took his hand while she soothed him. "Of course not. You are in no way bound to honour your aunt's wishes. Even if she and your mother planned a cradle match, it was not in writing or signed by your father. It is certainly not an obligation. You do not owe Miss de Bourgh your hand, but you *do* owe her the courtesy of an explanation. She should hear the words from your own lips. We must prevent a break in the family, which I can assure you would likely happen if the first Lady Catherine hears of it is through rumour."

Darcy remained silent, clearly unable to think of anything civil to say.

"You do understand I can read your thoughts," Elizabeth said gently. "You are wondering why your aunt's demands are your problem. I wish to correct your thinking. They are our problem, now and in our future life together. Whatever your aunt is, she does not deserve to read about our engagement in the paper. Do you understand why I have resisted coming to Darcy House for dinner? I do not want your aunt or my mother to learn about us through hearsay. It is not fair, and we would suffer the consequences of our indolence."

Elizabeth was too focused on her beau and worried about his feelings to notice anybody else, so she was startled to hear the colonel laugh heartily.

"She has you there, Cousin. You may as well admit defeat gracefully."

Georgiana voiced curiosity as to the need for the colonel and herself to accompany them to Rosings.

After looking to ensure that Darcy was not having an apoplexy, Elizabeth turned to Georgiana. "Because you are no longer a child, and you should not be afraid of your aunt."

"You and I have amends to make, Georgie. During my previous visit to Rosings, I *ignored* your cousin Anne. I did not pay her the slightest attention beyond the basic courtesies. I wish to rectify that. I believe you should do the same. How can you handle the *ton* if you are afraid of your own aunt and cousin? I have no idea what Anne's life is like, or if she wants it to be any different, but it is about to change dramatically.

She should have the support of someone besides her mother when it happens."

Georgiana looked a bit frightened but resolute, which was good enough for Elizabeth. She returned her attention to Darcy, who was gazing at her with such warm intensity that she wondered whether he might kiss her right there in the Gardiner's sunny parlour.

After a moment admiring his expression, she said, rather weakly, "Also, there are other considerations."

Happily, Darcy understood quickly. "The Collinses? The living is for life, and Lady Catherine cannot take it away, but my aunt could make their situation uncomfortable," Darcy said ruefully.

"Yes. A stronger man would ignore your aunt, but my cousin would suffer exceedingly from the loss of her approbation. I would not like to see Charlotte affected adversely. We need to prevent that."

Darcy agreed, and Elizabeth, knowing him better than she ever expected, rapped affectionately on his head with her knuckles.

"One moment, please. There is one more point I want to make about the visit. All those reasons I have named are important, but they are not the main purpose of my desire to return to Rosings."

Darcy was not the only one who gazed at her intently. Everyone sat on the edge of their seats, waiting in suspense to hear what she had to say.

She laughed. "You may all relax. It is nothing so terrible. You see, surprising as it may be to some of you, I *like* Lady Catherine. She is a difficult person to be sure, but I must admit I have crossed the Rubicon. I would not like to hurt her any more than necessary. I want to keep her society.

"And besides all that, she does give a great deal of advice and much of it is quite good."

With that, all restraint was lost among the three visitors related to Lady Catherine. Mr and Mrs Gardiner joined in their laughter.

It would be some time before Darcy and Richard worked out that Elizabeth was entirely serious.

CHAPTER SEVENTEEN

Avalanche

ONCE DARCY REALISED THE TRIP TO ROSINGS WAS A prerequisite to showing off his lady publicly, he would have happily thrown her over his shoulder and left for Kent that very minute. That seemed precipitous, so they planned to go after one day of preparation. Darcy sent an express, giving fair warning to Lady Catherine that he would arrive with guests and expect to spend the night, although, if the discussion proceeded poorly, he thought he could arrange lodgings easily enough. It would not be the first or last time he arrived or left a place unexpectedly.

In his mind, the ideal would be to carry Elizabeth on his horse or in his smallest carriage or curricle the entire distance. Any other participants were a detriment to be left behind at the first opportunity. Surprisingly, Elizabeth's ideal plan would not have been so different. She had, by her own design, included Georgiana and the colonel, but as she confided to him, she was reconsidering her invitation even before their party expanded by two.

Jane said she did not want to be left in London, particularly when Darcy got word that the Bingleys were back in town and hoping for a visit. When Georgiana expressed a strong desire to have someone for her own support on a visit to her frightening aunt at Rosings, all was settled.

Mr Gardiner expressed his belief that two unmarried ladies under his protection travelling with two highly eligible bachelors seemed a bit too far beyond the bounds of propriety—particularly when one of said gentleman looked ready to make for Gretna Green at the slightest provocation. He assigned himself to the journey as chaperon, bringing the party to six. They expected to return within the two days Mr Gardiner could afford to be away from his business.

The trip itself was fairly boisterous, and the time passed easily. Darcy was happy to see that Georgiana and Jane got along very well. He continued to behave akin to what the colonel had asserted was his true character—lively enough in other places—and he sensed Elizabeth's appreciation.

All was well as they neared Rosings. When Elizabeth saw the parsonage, her posture stiffened, and she gave Darcy a faint smile.

A few minutes later, the gentlemen handed down the ladies to an empty drive. No insult was intended, Darcy assured Mr Gardiner and the Bennet sisters. Lady Catherine believed her parlour was where visitors should be greeted. However, without even a footman to meet them, the dowager would be unaware of the number and identities of her guests until they entered the room where she awaited them. He had been less than explicit in his express.

Darcy pulled Elizabeth aside for a private conversation. "Before we enter, I must state the obvious. Our understanding will be fully public after this. I know you have been wary, but I have not wished to be. I hope you know that."

"Of course. You are a man of extremes. You either show nothing at all or everything. Your intentions have been clear enough since your conversation with Jane and me."

"Does that trouble you?"

Elizabeth smiled somewhat shyly and glanced down. "Not anymore. In fact, I rather like it. You know what you want and work to achieve it without relying on subterfuge, dishonesty, or underhanded tricks. It is an admirable trait."

"Admirable in general or—"

She laughed gaily while wagging a finger at him. "No fishing for compliments, sir. I can assure you that if a trait was admirable in the general sense, but I did not admire it in you specifically, I would find another word. I have an excellent vocabulary."

"That you do," he said and wondered how in the world he was to get through another five weeks without kissing her.

Elizabeth's laughter waned. "Before we go in, I would ask something of you. Obviously, you will introduce the topic of our courtship, but would you allow me to do most of the talking?"

"Naturally! In fact, I am of a mind to take everyone else to the parsonage for a few hours and collect you when you are finished. I am certain Mrs Collins can accommodate us."

Elizabeth swatted his arm.

Darcy grew serious. "I only wish you to understand something important before we enter."

"Now?"

He smiled nervously. It was rare to have a completely private conversation with the lady he loved, and while their companions were gawking at the splendour of Rosings, he had words he longed to say.

"Yes, now! It may become important as we discuss matters with my aunt."

Darcy looked at her with what he hoped was affection in his expression, pressed the small hands he mysteriously found in his own to his chest, and said gently, "I wish to make something clear, Elizabeth. On the thirteenth of April, at a quarter past four by Mr Gardiner's clock, you accepted a two-month courtship. I have been inordinately happy with how our understanding is progressing, and I can assure you that, absent a clear and strong objection on your part, on the thirteenth of June at precisely a quarter past four, I shall offer you my hand in marriage. I shall not be dissuaded from offering, although the final choice to accept will obviously be yours."

She blushed becomingly before saying archly, "But you have not endured the Longbourn portion of your labours."

"Do you seriously believe your mother will be any more intimidating than my aunt, your father more teasing and impertinent than Richard, or your younger sisters any more taxing than the Bingleys? There is nothing they could do short of coming at me with an axe that would check me."

"I should probably refrain from telling you that the idea of kissing you is nowhere near as abhorrent as it once was."

Warmth flooded him, and he smiled sweetly at her. "I shall take it under advisement. Shall we?"

He offered her his arm, she took it without qualms, and they went to brace the dragon in her den.

The butler, Mr Greaves, finally emerged to welcome the group to Rosings and addressed Darcy. "Her ladyship has guests in the parlour, sir. Would you care to wait?"

Suspecting that being in company with a few of his aunt's cronies might mitigate her response slightly, Darcy asked Greaves to announce their party.

It did not occur to him to ask who the guests were. Lady Catherine did not entertain often, and Darcy was familiar with most of her friends. His aunt preferred to maintain the distinction of rank, so he knew most of the people in her domain were practically vassals in her mind.

Greaves raised his eyebrows fractionally at his answer, but he pushed the doors open and made the announcement of their arrival.

With some surprise, Darcy realised his aunt must have been in some kind of altercation. Her colour was high, and she appeared as agitated as Darcy had ever seen her. The grand lady snapped her attention to the group, and he saw the moment she made some incorrect assumptions. He had brought a larger party and assumed that beyond her anger at that presumption, she would be furious when she learnt Mr Gardiner was in trade. In the brief moment before he gave his full attention to Lady Catherine, Darcy noticed Mr Gardiner wearing an impertinent grin that reminded him very much of his Elizabeth, and he had to admire the man's composure.

Darcy bowed to his aunt. "Good afternoon, Lady Catherine. I trust we are not disturbing your day."

Without asking for an introduction or explanation, Darcy was surprised when she launched into a tirade.

"You ought to know I am not to be trifled with, Darcy," her ladyship cried in an angry tone. "However insincere you may choose to be, you will not find me so. My character has ever been celebrated for its sincerity and frankness, and in a cause of such moment as this, I shall certainly not depart from it.

"A report of a most alarming nature reached me not five minutes ago. I was told that your present companion, Miss Elizabeth Bennet, would in all likelihood, be soon afterwards united to you, my own nephew. I know it to be a scandalous falsehood. Although I would not injure you so much as to suppose the truth of it possible, I instantly resolved on finding you, that I might make my sentiments known. I see you have saved me the trouble. I was resolved to go to London this very afternoon."

Completely at a loss as to how his aunt might have learnt of his current situation, Darcy focused entirely on his adversary, not even bothering to look at her visitors.

"If you believed it impossible to be true," said Darcy, colouring with astonishment and disdain at the sheer rudeness his aunt was exhibiting, "I wonder you planned to take the trouble of coming so far. What could your ladyship propose by it?"

"To insist upon having such a report universally contradicted."

"By coming to London to see me," said Darcy coolly, barely in regulation of his temper, "you would have rather confirmed it. In fact, had you done so publicly, you could well have raised enough eyebrows to *oblige* me if the purpose of your visit became generally known."

Ignoring his assertion that her actions could well have caused what she apparently so strenuously sought to avoid, his aunt continued in some astonishment.

"If! *If!* Do you then pretend to be ignorant? Do you not know that such a report is spread abroad?"

"I never heard that it was."

"And can you likewise declare there is no foundation for it?"

Becoming quite agitated, Darcy felt Elizabeth squeeze his arm with the apparent aim of keeping his temper in check.

Much to his surprise, it was Jane who stepped into the breach. "Mr Darcy," she said in a gentle tone that was far harder to ignore than a shout.

He turned to look at her, and she gave him a slightly arched eyebrow that could well have been a sign reading, *Remember your manners.*

Sufficiently chastened, Darcy finally looked around the room and was stunned to see the last people he ever expected to appear in Lady Catherine's house. In fact, he was surprised the grand lady had allowed them into Rosings at all, let alone into her parlour.

Elizabeth shared not only Darcy's surprise at seeing Miss Bingley and Mrs Hurst in Lady Catherine's parlour, but his dismay at how their own party had been received. She could but imagine how Jane must have felt, already a bit at sea in this over-furnished house. Seeing the dowager ready to jump on whatever Darcy said next, Elizabeth was pleased that he moved to calm the situation.

Darcy acknowledged Jane's reproof. "You are correct, Miss Bennet. Where are my manners? Perhaps I should perform introductions?"

"That seems wise," Elizabeth said in a voice befitting the tense atmosphere before anybody could gainsay him.

"Lady Catherine de Bourgh, may I present some acquaintances. This is Mr Edwin Gardiner, uncle to the Bennet sisters."

Mr Gardiner bowed, showing perfect good breeding—or it would have been, without the slight smirk he gave Elizabeth that disclosed his enjoyment of the show. Elizabeth wondered at how similar her father and her uncle were and sighed, thinking that she had a perfectly good excuse for her own impertinence.

"A pleasure, Lady Catherine. My niece Elizabeth has told me a great deal about you, and her *praise* was not exaggerated, I can see."

Elizabeth wondered what praise her uncle was talking about, but she thought calling him to task on the assertion would be pointless.

Lady Catherine seemed somewhat mollified, particularly since Darcy had cleverly introduced the subterfuge of making Mr Gardiner seem of higher rank than he held. Darcy suspected his aunt would be furious when she found him to be a tradesman.

Not wanting to spend all day in introductions, Darcy followed the established order.

"Lady Catherine, most of your guests are already acquainted with Colonel Fitzwilliam. May I also present Miss Bennet of Longbourn in Hertfordshire, and her sister Miss Elizabeth, whom you already know. Miss Georgiana Darcy is already known to you and most of my party know Mrs Hurst and Miss Bingley. Ladies and gentlemen, your host and my aunt, Lady Catherine de Bourgh."

It was lost on no one that Caroline Bingley was the lowest-ranked person in the room. Elizabeth stared at her coldly, as though daring her to contradict Darcy for introducing Mr Gardiner before her.

Miss Bingley stepped closer to Darcy, a victorious expression on her face.

"The report to which Lady Catherine refers came from me. I heard accounts that the Miss Bennets had applied their arts and allurements to bring you under their power. I sought out Lady Catherine to try to make matters right."

With a frightful glare, Darcy asked, "I wonder how this report of a very private matter might have come to your attention, Miss Bingley. Do you have spies tracking my movements?"

The lady started to reply, but Jane spoke first.

"I suggest caution, Miss Bingley. Things said now cannot be retracted. A confession must be dealt with, but a mere implication or suspicion might later be ignored."

Elizabeth could only admire her sister's display of cool surety, especially as Jane turned to address Lady Catherine.

"It is a great pleasure to meet you, my lady, but I wonder if I might be excused for a few minutes. I believe you have learnt all you need to from the Bingley sisters, while Colonel Fitzwilliam and I have other pressing business to discuss with the…ladies before they depart."

The colonel glanced at Jane with more than a little admiration in his eyes, and Elizabeth began to wonder at his feelings for her most worthy sister. Then, as the dowager's face reddened, Elizabeth could see the man's military background emerge, and he took Jane's request as orders.

He gave a sweeping bow reminiscent of Mr Collins and announced, "We shall return momentarily, Aunt. Perhaps you could call for tea?"

Lady Catherine sputtered and looked slightly confused as the colonel latched onto Miss Bingley's arm, and Mr Gardiner did the same to Mrs Hurst. Both men met with some resistance by the sisters as they were conveyed out of the room. With a smile and a deep curtsey, Jane took Georgiana's arm and followed.

Only Elizabeth and Darcy remained.

CHAPTER EIGHTEEN

Beached Fish

"CLOSE YOUR MOUTH, NEPHEW. YOU RESEMBLE A BEACHED fish," Lady Catherine said with some asperity.

Darcy belatedly closed his mouth and turned back. "Where were we?"

"You were about to contradict universally the rumour concerning an attachment between the two of you."

"Will you allow me to answer, Lady Catherine?" Elizabeth asked sweetly.

The great lady's expression made her look as though she were sucking lemons, but she grudgingly replied, "As you wish."

Elizabeth thought Darcy's aunt must be quite discomposed because they were her first words not spoken as though she expected it to amaze the whole room and be handed down to posterity with all the éclat of a proverb.

As Elizabeth opened her mouth to speak, Miss Anne de Bourgh stepped into the room.

The presence of the young heiress discomfited Elizabeth. She had spent many weeks in Kent wedded to her first impressions so strongly that she never made the slightest effort to befriend the sickly looking young woman.

"Cousin, Miss Bennet! What a pleasure it is to see you again!"

It was the most Elizabeth had ever heard the young lady say, so she smiled and curtseyed. "It is good to see you, Miss de Bourgh."

"Anne, please join us. This discussion affects you," Darcy added.

Lady Catherine started to speak, but Darcy forestalled her by raising his hand. "You agreed to let Miss Elizabeth speak, madam."

Anne perked up at the subtle hint. "Oh, is your elder sister present as well?" she said with a smile that briefly surprised Elizabeth, but then she surmised that since Rosings must be the most tedious place on Earth, perhaps the young lady wanted company.

"Yes, she is here and hopes to meet you. She is engaged in some business with Colonel Fitzwilliam and Miss Darcy just now. With your permission, we shall introduce her soon."

Anne's face lit up in a smile that again discomposed Elizabeth. She wondered whether such a smile had been available all along, but as with her cousin Darcy, her countenance did not usually display such frivolity. It was a matter that would have to be considered later, Elizabeth decided. She had more urgent business.

Elizabeth took a deep breath, let go of Darcy's arm, and took a step forward. "Lady Catherine, if I may be allowed to continue."

Darcy's aunt still looked quite put out. "Go on! I shall not stop you."

"When we last spoke in April, I was not prevaricating. It

was my firmest conviction that Mr Darcy and I shared a mutual dislike of some intensity and duration. I asked your assistance to leave Rosings specifically to avoid him."

Lady Catherine looked at her carefully. "This sounds like more arts and allurements."

"If you consider frowns, impertinence, and trying my best to wound with nearly every word as arts and allurements, I shall concede to your definition, although perhaps your nephew was simply sick of people who always played to his vanity. I can assure you it was most unconsciously done."

"I admit if it was a strategy, it was well chosen. A good warrior knows that trying the same tactic that everyone else employs and finds unsuccessful is generally ineffective."

"But I did not choose it, Lady Catherine. I would beg you to believe that securing his good opinion was the furthest thing from my mind when I left Rosings."

"What happened? More importantly, will you finally be explicit?"

Elizabeth looked back to Darcy. "It seems the dislike was unevenly distributed."

"Meaning?"

"Meaning it was all on my side. Part of it was based on his occasionally atrocious manners, part was based on some well-meaning but destructive interference in my sister's life, and part was based on some wildly incorrect information I believed without verification from a liar and a scoundrel. Mr Darcy came to my uncle's house in London, explained himself, apologised, and set out to correct those wrongs."

"I suppose he felt honour-bound to do so?"

"Can you doubt it?" Elizabeth smiled at the silent man beside her.

Lady Catherine also looked at Darcy, who seemed entirely

happy to leave the discussion to them, and then at her daughter, who was listening in apparent fascination.

"Nephew, I presume you and Fitzwilliam somehow learnt of this. How did it come about?"

Darcy shifted on his feet. "Richard learnt Miss Elizabeth believed we disliked each other quite by chance, and I corrected him. I had interfered in affairs that were none of my business, to the detriment of both Miss Bennet and my friend Bingley. I also failed to do my duty as a gentleman with respect to George Wickham."

"I have no idea why your father doted on that reprobate. He should have been drowned at birth," Lady Catherine said sharply with a frown.

Elizabeth was surprised by both the vehemence of the declaration and Lady Catherine's apparent comfort with her assessment.

Darcy said, "Be that as it may, Wickham has found his calling in the navy."

Miss de Bourgh, whose presence had been mostly forgotten, surprised everyone by speaking up. "Did he see the light, Cousin?"

"He was shown the light," was all Darcy was willing to say, although the implication was obvious.

Miss de Bourgh once again surprised everyone by asking sweetly, "Shall we stop prevaricating and diverting? Say what you came all this way to say."

Taking a deep breath, Elizabeth began. "We all know Lady Catherine believes you and Mr Darcy have a cradle engagement. I have heard it spoken of often enough, inside and outside of Rosings, and even in Hertfordshire. I suspect Mr Darcy, honourable as he is, would have taken his mother and aunt's wishes into consideration. It is perfectly just and natural that a mother and her sister should think of a match for their children. Every mother I ever met started thinking about matches long before such plans were necessary. However this plan was formed, its completion depended on others. If Mr Darcy is neither by honour nor inclination confined to Miss de Bourgh, why is he not free to make another choice? For that matter, he cannot even be assured of a positive response to an offer made to Miss de Bourgh."

Elizabeth had been slowly walking towards Lady Catherine, speaking softly so as not to appear overly eager, and was but three feet away from the lady.

"Lady Catherine, Miss de Bourgh. Mr Darcy has asked to court me, and I have accepted. We are not engaged, but the chances of that coming to pass increase every day."

Quite to her surprise, the younger woman jumped from her chair and moved swiftly across the few feet that separated them. She ran past her cousin, threw her arms around a thoroughly flabbergasted Elizabeth, and cried, "Oh bless you! Bless you! I am so happy!"

Even more astounding, Elizabeth found herself being lifted off her feet as Anne hugged her for dear life. She fell back on a long-established habit when in the company of exuberant females and reached around to return the hug, but ideally, without the potential for injury that Elizabeth was suffering from herself.

"Apparently, this makes you happy, Miss de Bourgh?"

"We are to be cousins! Might you call me Anne?"

Lady Catherine stared at them in shock. Elizabeth gave the lady a questioning look, which received no more than a shrug in answer. She glanced at Darcy, who looked as stunned as she felt. Elizabeth could not look at Anne's face, since it was attached to her shoulder as though nailed there.

"I may be your cousin in a few months. We must not put the cart before the horse, but I would be honoured to call you Anne. You may call me Elizabeth or Lizzy. Whether I accept your cousin or not, I would like to know you better."

Lady Catherine looked defeated. "Is this the last word on the subject, Nephew? It seems the tides are against me."

"Not necessarily, Mama," Miss de Bourgh said. "I think now that we have clarity, I can admit I do not wish to marry at all. At the very least, I do not want to have children. I am sure we can devise something better. I have some ideas."

Lady Catherine appeared dubious. "If you have such good ideas, why is this the first I have heard of them?"

"I wanted Darcy out of contention. I believe he has been using our supposed cradle engagement as a shield for many years, at least in his own mind. I did not object, as it served my purposes, but with him marrying—"

"*Courting!*" Elizabeth cried.

"Yes, yes, courting and then, marrying. Now is the time. Before was not."

"Lady Catherine, I understand the desire to combine your estates, but I doubt it was ever wise if you consider the future." Elizabeth gently said.

Darcy, who had played no role in the conversation beyond guiding his cousin and Elizabeth to seats near his aunt, spoke up. "What do you mean, Elizabeth?"

Her cheeks pinked. "Forgive my lack of delicacy, but the problem with the plan was one of fecundity."

"Excuse me!" cried Lady Catherine.

"Suppose Anne did marry her cousin and combined the estates. This vast area, thousands of tenants and dependents spread across two counties, would depend on the fertility of one woman. It would be all or nothing. If she could not produce an heir, all would come crashing down. It is far more sensible to cut the risk in half by delegating the creation of the next generation to two women. It is nothing but common sense."

All three stared at her for a moment, until Darcy started chuckling. He finally said, "It takes you, my dear, to speak such common sense aloud. I wish I had thought to say it a decade ago."

Lady Catherine said, "Do you truly believe you would have dissuaded me with common sense, Nephew?"

"No, I suppose not."

"I know you think your nephew offering for me would be a degradation, Lady Catherine. I believe he thought that way himself a fortnight ago."

Darcy seemed chagrined but did not contradict Elizabeth, and Lady Catherine appeared in agreement.

"Mr Darcy is a gentleman. I am a gentleman's daughter. By the rules of society, we are equals as we are both the children of gentlemen. My family lacks the wealth of Mr Darcy, but the Bennets have held Longbourn for more than two hundred years."

Darcy said quietly, "Elizabeth and I meet as equals."

Admitting defeat gracefully was difficult after a quarter-century dream, but Lady Catherine was nothing if not resilient. "I can see little profit in pushing against the tides. If you two make a match, I shall give my blessing, for what it is worth."

"It is worth a great deal, madam. You are the only sister of my late, beloved mother." Darcy gave the dowager a warm smile, which she attempted to return. "It may surprise you to learn that Elizabeth insisted on this trip most strenuously. You can imagine I would have been happy to write you a letter, or worse yet, let you learn about it when it became public knowledge. It was *she* who demanded we tell you personally. *She* insisted you be the first in the family to know. Other than Georgiana, Elizabeth's aunt and uncle, and those two harridans who are presently learning the error of their ways from Richard and Miss Bennet, you are the first to be informed."

"Why, Elizabeth?" Miss de Bourgh asked.

"Real or imagined, the cradle engagement has been a part of your lives for quite some time. It would not be right to make you learn about it second-hand, and I am sorry it came from the source it did."

Very surprisingly, Lady Catherine said, "Bah! It is in the past."

Anne and Darcy smiled at each other, and Elizabeth thought it a heartening sign before she made a request she had not mentioned to Darcy.

"In addition, I wish to ask a favour of you, my lady. I could hardly do that if we did not show you the basic respect of informing you of our courtship ourselves."

"What sort of favour?" Lady Catherine asked. Elizabeth thought her countenance lit up at the chance to do something useful.

Elizabeth wished to ensure privacy as the awkwardness of her request weighed on her. "This stays between us?" she whispered.

The lady agreed, and Elizabeth continued. "You will meet my sister in a few moments. Jane is grace and decorum personified."

"I can attest to that," Darcy added.

"My mother and my two youngest sisters are quite the opposite." Elizabeth looked down in embarrassment.

Lady Catherine asked gently, "You wish me to educate them?"

"I would be honoured if you would try. You were helpful to me when we last met. I hope I do not offend you by saying that many consider you..." She paused, carefully trying to find the appropriate words.

Lady Catherine helped her. "Controlling? overbearing?" Lady Catherine chuckled. "I can do better, Elizabeth. May I call you that?"

"Of course, my lady. Most in my family call me Lizzy, but I cannot imagine that name gracing your lips."

"You are quite correct, I assure you," Lady Catherine replied. "Now, tell me about your mother."

"She is the daughter of a tradesman who was never properly trained to be a lady. She is of mean understanding and uncertain temper, but I have never doubted her love for her family. Although she appears at times mercenary, at the root, she is just afraid. She is both fearful of and frustrated by the entail on my father's estate, so getting her daughters disposed of in marriage has been her life's goal. She does not know how to go about it, and most of her schemes are misguided, but she does try."

Anne asked, "I am curious, Lizzy. How do you know she is not mercenary?"

Elizabeth grinned and reached for Darcy's hand. "Your cousin slighted me the first night we were in company. Within my hearing, he said I was not handsome enough to tempt him to dance. My mother took an instant dislike to him, discouraged me from dancing with him in future, and proceeded to disparage him to the entire neighbourhood."

Darcy's full attention took hold at that revelation.

"Did you fail to notice that no one in Meryton threw their daughters at your feet after that first assembly?" Elizabeth asked.

Darcy was silent for a moment, and finally, with a grin, said, "Of course I would have noticed if I was not so thoroughly distracted."

Elizabeth had no idea what to say to that, especially since his eyes were dark and intense, and she now knew it was not in disapproval.

Elizabeth felt as though they had just won a great victory. She was especially pleased to think it was she and Darcy who accomplished it. They had done it as a couple. It was becoming increasingly difficult to think of spending a day or tackling any problem without him.

It was food for thought or was that food for love, or was that music or poetry? She chuckled at her silliness and could not wait to get Mr Darcy alone so she could tease him about it.

CHAPTER NINETEEN

Ducks and Swans

MISS ELSMITH'S SEMINARY FOR YOUNG LADIES TAUGHT THEIR pupils that a lady should glide along, neck held high, arms positioned just so, feet moving slowly and invisibly, taking the elegant swan as a model.

At Rosings, Caroline Bingley was learning the difficult lesson that it was very hard to glide like a swan when you were being dragged out of the parlour by a cavalryman who thought shooting people was a better than average solution to many of life's little inconveniences.

While the ignominious exit was occurring, Mrs Hurst seemed to at least recognise a lost cause. She took Mr Gardiner's arm when it was offered and moved along without complaint. Jane and Georgiana walked regally behind them, diverted by the colonel's manoeuvres. The group in the entrance hall came to an abrupt halt when the front door burst open to reveal the arrival of yet another unexpected visitor.

"Bingley!" Fitzwilliam called out. "Come join the party! We have much to discuss."

Bingley, clearly shocked by the colonel's presence, gave out a jovial response. "Colonel! Well met, sir!"

Turning more serious, he continued, "It seems you know more of what is happening than I do. I received word that my sisters travelled here abruptly and without invitation. I thought the chances of mischief seemed high, so I came to see what kind of predicament they got into this time."

The colonel watched in amusement as realisation dawned on Bingley, and he espied the two women he had been pursuing, both clearly unhappy, uncomfortable, and being held firmly by himself and Mr Gardiner.

Miss Bingley started to speak, but a slight squeeze of her arm was enough to quiet her. He felt her shudder. Clearly, she understood her brother's presence could only worsen her situation.

In the authoritative tone he used on the battlefield when ordering to run towards cannon fire, Colonel Fitzwilliam said, "Bingley, we have serious matters to discuss, including how you manage your household—or fail to do so, as appears to be the case."

Bingley stood a bit straighter. "Excuse me?"

The colonel waved to the butler, who had been hovering discreetly about ten feet out of hearing range.

"Greaves, we shall retire to the grey parlour," the colonel said and then thoroughly enjoyed the closest thing to shock he had ever seen on the butler's face.

Fitzwilliam had been trying to discompose the man since he was a boy, and this was his best effort yet. He was hoping to get Greaves to ask if he was entirely certain, but he was to be once again disappointed.

"I shall make certain it is ready, Colonel."

As the butler left to make arrangements, Bingley asked, "Would you introduce me to your companion?" as though this was an ordinary drawing-room conversation.

"Mr Gardiner of Gracechurch Street, may I present Mr Bingley of…Netherfield? London? Scarborough?"

If Bingley understood the disdain in the colonel's question about his residence, he ignored it. "Mr Gardiner, I am pleased to meet you. I had some acquaintances in Hertfordshire with an uncle who lived somewhere near Cheapside. Perhaps you are acquainted with them. They are the Miss Ben—"

Before he could complete the name, Jane stepped out from behind the group, causing Bingley to cut off mid-word with a strangled sound, and stare at her with his mouth hanging slightly open. Five months had certainly not done Jane's appearance any disservice, and in fact, the case could be made that she looked quite beautiful when angry.

"Mr Gardiner is my uncle, sir. I am afraid I do not have enough uncles to fill all of Cheapside— just the one."

Bingley startled at the appearance of his angel, but once he was over his initial shock, his face lit up in a broad smile, and he bowed deeply.

"Miss Bennet, it is the greatest of possible pleasures to see you aga–"

"You cannot be serious!" Jane retorted.

Bingley had made the greeting out of habit, thoroughly ignoring the fact that Jane appeared angry. She also apparently had access to what was said in her absence at Netherfield.

Her reaction, on the other hand, may have lacked specificity, but it certainly did not lack sentiment. She was not in the least happy to see him.

Bingley was quite taken aback and confused. The fact that

Jane was even capable of anger was a surprise, and having it directed at him instead of his sisters thoroughly unsettled him.

Finally, he stuttered. "I do not understand."

The colonel shook his head. "You most certainly do not understand quite a number of things. We shall do our best to enlighten you but not here!"

Greaves appeared at the same time with a similar aim. "Right this way, if you please," he asked, gesturing down the hall.

Bingley offered his arm to Miss Bennet, but she looked at it with a curled lip, then pointedly ignored it in favour of taking Georgiana's.

They climbed a grand staircase. Most of the group, especially the Bingley sisters, appeared somewhat less enamoured of its grandeur with the second, third, and fourth flights of stairs. They had lost their ladylike manner and were gasping for breath and sweating. Ten minutes later, even Mr Gardiner was mopping his brow, and Miss Bennet was slightly less composed than usual. The colonel was accustomed to a far more strenuous life, and Georgiana had spent years climbing up and down the peaks of Derbyshire, so they were not bothered by the exercise.

Greaves, breathing heavily, led them into the grey parlour. It was the most hideous room at Rosings, and a good case could be made for it being the most unattractive parlour in England. The room, which had not been redecorated since the seven-teenth century, was furnished with costly but terribly ugly and uncomfortable pieces. Over the years and generations, it was occasionally resurrected for its original purpose of intimi-dating one's opponents, and the colonel thought to do the same now with the Bingleys, although more for his own amusement than tactical advantage.

Everyone looked around nervously, and Colonel Fitzwilliam wondered if he might have made a mistake when Georgiana looked even more frightened than Jane. Now that he had recovered from the journey up the stairs, Mr Gardiner looked amused. Miss Bingley was staring wide-eyed at the décor, so the colonel wondered if he could tell her it was to be next year's fashion and convince her to redecorate Hurst's townhouse in a similar style.

The colonel asked everyone to sit, but pointedly did not call for refreshments before launching into his business.

"Bingley, Miss Bingley, Mrs Hurst. Let me start by saying that we had plans to speak to all of you within the week. We believe we have some offences to discuss with each of you. Your sisters' uncalled-for and extremely impertinent interfer-ence here just advanced the discussion a few days. You were in disfavour already."

Miss Bingley, perched on a settee the colonel knew was as comfortable as a bed of nails, said coldly, "You can have nothing to say to us, sir. Our business is with Lady Catherine, who welcomed us graciously into her lovely home. She would not have us dragged up six floors, virtually manhandled like—"

Colonel Fitzwilliam interrupted her forcefully. "You do not want to finish that sentence, Miss Bingley. The comparisons to a fishwife or a prisoner being dragged to gaol are not what you want to be under serious consideration."

Caroline Bingley recoiled, turned red in fury, and started to speak again, but before she could further anger her assailants, she was quite forcefully overridden by her brother.

"For once in your life, Caroline, do be quiet. I wager you have put us in enough trouble as it is without making it worse. I, for one, want to hear what charges the colonel has against you without interruptions."

Jane gave him a cross look. "You are very much mistaken if you think your sister is the only one in the dock here, Mr Bingley."

Georgiana touched her lightly on her arm. "Jane, may I speak?" she asked, all politeness.

Jane appeared astonished by the request, but she adopted her previous, calmer demeanour. "Of course, Georgiana." She turned to look at the colonel. "As Georgiana's guardian, do you agree, Richard?"

All three of the Bingley siblings startled to hear Jane Bennet use the given names of the sister of Fitzwilliam Darcy and the second son of the Earl of Matlock.

The colonel smiled. "Go ahead, Georgie. I can wait my turn," he drawled in a threatening tone of voice that implied that when his turn came, unpleasant scenes might arise.

Georgiana smiled sweetly, looking for all the world the timid little mouse she had been a few months prior. "Jane, please give the letter to Mr Bingley."

Jane extracted the letter from her reticule and handed it to the gentleman. "Do not worry about exchanging correspondence with me," Jane assured him. "That letter was written to me by your sister."

Bingley slowly opened the missive, his expression wary.

"How dare you share private correspondence!" Miss Bingley cried out.

Unperturbed, Georgiana replied serenely. "You are not the

injured party, and you never made reference to this being a private matter." She turned to Mr Bingley. "Pray carry on, sir."

Appearing thoroughly confused, Bingley began reading the letter. His expression changed quickly to fury. He stared at his sister in disbelief and thundered, "You wrote this? That I was courting Miss Darcy? When? Why?"

Georgiana answered for her. "She had this delivered the day after the Netherfield ball. In other words, she delivered it as you were on the road to London, after telling Jane you would return in a few days."

She turned to Miss Bingley, whose countenance remained twisted in anger. "Do you deny it? Do you deny that you, publicly and in writing, toyed with the reputation of a sixteen-year-old girl who is not even out, by asserting an attachment to your brother, who had just spent six weeks calling on and raising expectations in my dear friend Jane?"

Miss Bingley looked stunned by the turn of events. Colonel Fitzwilliam was duly impressed by his cousin's inter-rogation, but Georgiana was not quite finished with the lady.

"This is not to be borne! A lady's reputation is her most precious commodity, and you, Miss Bingley, were entirely too willing to be reckless with mine! *Answer me!*"

CHAPTER TWENTY

Growing Up

MISS BINGLEY'S CONTROL SLIPPED AND REVEALED HER ANGER. "I have no wish to deny it. Nothing written there is untrue, and there is nothing untoward in hoping for the match. Every mother and sister in England would do the same, and Mrs Bennet did far worse within an hour of meeting our party. If you object to my ambitions but absolve Mrs Bennet—well, I have no idea what to think."

Colonel Fitzwilliam had been watching his ward carefully to see how she handled the unpleasant and vitriolic Miss Bingley. He knew full well that Georgiana would be subject to that same kind of woman and worse when she came out in society. This seemed as good a time as any to help strengthen her resolve. He nodded to her in support, and she returned her attention to Miss Bingley.

"Blaming others for your own actions is childish…unsurprisingly. Let us disregard for the moment the damage you were doing to my reputation and that of Jane and your brother."

The colonel looked at Bingley and saw a terrible combination of confusion, anger, and impotence. He had started out being taken to task by Jane Bennet, the gentlest and kindest woman in the world. Then he graduated to being upbraided by Georgiana Darcy, the shyest and most timid girl of his acquaintance.

The boy just cannot win, the colonel thought, biting back a chuckle.

Georgiana persisted. "Mrs Bennet, whom I am reliably informed is the most prolific gossip in Meryton, could easily have seen this note. Jane received it and read it at their break-fast table. Can you imagine what would happen if rumours of your brother and me had spread to—"

She paused a moment as though she had just answered the question herself. The colonel could see the moment when the implications became clear, and Georgiana's expression clouded in anger and her jaw clenched.

"Oh my! That is what you intended, was it not, Miss Bing-ley? A damaging association was not an unfortunate and unforeseen consequence of your effort to hurt Jane. It was not an accident. It was by design! You hoped to have your brother *obliged* to me."

Miss Bingley tried to dissuade the young girl. "No, it was not by design. How could you think that? Mr Darcy and I were close friends and becoming closer all the time. It was obvious to all, and it was natural to assume—"

"Bite your tongue!" Jane cried, startling everyone.

In the dead silence following her outburst, the colonel glanced at Mr Gardiner. The man who had known Jane Bennet since she was born appeared as stunned as the rest of the party.

Remarkably, Jane continued in her usual sweet, complaisant voice. "Thank you, Georgiana. That was enlight-ening. If you have no objection, I shall take my turn now."

"By all means," Georgiana replied with a slight smile.

"You have known Fitzwilliam Darcy for some five years. I have known him for eight weeks, but I can assure you that I know him far better than you ever will. You have been proceeding under the delusion that he might either offer for you eventually or that you could somehow contrive a compromise."

Everyone gasped, but the colonel knew Darcy always locked the door to his chambers at any house in which he was in residence with Miss Bingley. Had she got into his rooms— into his bed— she would have been gravely disappointed.

Darcy would have packed up, gone to town, stopped by White's to observe who collected on the bets wagered about when and how the chit would ruin herself, and gone about his business.

Jane continued in a cool, measured voice.

"He will not, nor has he ever planned to offer for you. He would not mind my telling you his sentiments. He had not known you a month before he felt that you were the last woman in the world whom he could ever be prevailed on to marry. He has tolerated your company out of his friendship with your brother."

Mr Bingley and his sisters all began to sputter their displeasure, but Jane continued softly. "It is a shame, really, Miss Bingley. You were gifted with beauty, money, education, connexions—everything a woman could dream of—but all of it is tarnished by greed. I should hate you, but I do not. I pity you, for you threw it all away for *nothing*."

Without waiting for an answer, she turned to her former

favourite. "Mr Bingley, my strongest feeling about our association is one of shame. At two and twenty, I was as naïve as my youngest sister, Lydia. You came into the neighbourhood with your expensive clothes, expensive manners, and jovial disposition, and I was drawn in. I feel so very stupid now. Darcy thought me unmoved because I did not fawn all over you, but I would say I showed you the exact amount of affection a lady is *supposed* to show. Perhaps I was at fault, but I think not."

She stared at him as though he were on exhibit at the Royal Society and continued. "You left for 'a few days' and then had your sister, who you knew disparaged any connexion to the Bennets, write to me.

"And then you just gave me up. You allowed Fitzwilliam Darcy, a man whom I now respect and care for dearly as my future brother but who is quite ignorant about women, convince you that I did not care for you. You took his word, based on observations of a few hours from a distance, over *your own judgment* during six weeks of somewhat intimate and often private conversation."

She shuddered in apparent revulsion. "I have forgiven Darcy. Although he was supremely misguided, he gave his counsel in the service of a friend. You, however, acted from lack of resolution and courage, unlike your sister who acts out of malice and spite. It is an improvement but a slight one."

Bingley began to fight back. "So, Miss Bennet! Your contention is that the end of our association is all my fault—or mine and my sister's. You must admit that Darcy's observations were essentially correct. I always thought you gave me particular attention, but I realise now you gave the same attention and smiles to everyone. Darcy said your mother would try to force an attachment regardless of your affection, which has been proved to be correct. I heard about Mr Collins—about how Miss Elizabeth rejected his proposal, and your mother tried to force her—as she would have done with me given the chance. I shall take my share of the blame but not all."

Jane looked at him pityingly. "Did Darcy tell you to abandon me without taking your leave? Did he instruct you not to act in a gentlemanlike manner? Did he tell you a lady would make her affections obvious to any observer in a public setting? I shall at least agree that you had no obligation to offer for me, but you most certainly owed me an explanation. All you had to do was read Miss Bingley's letter before she sent it or take your leave properly."

Mr Bingley growled in frustration. "And I was supposed to ignore your mother's words? Mrs Bennet spent an hour at supper talking about how you would be mistress of Netherfield by Christmas, even though I had known you but a few weeks. What of her discussions about how many jewels and carriages you would have, or how much your pin money would be, or how lovely it would be to have her daughter so well settled and so close to home, or how I would be responsible for throwing your sisters in the paths of other rich men? Should I have *ignored* all of that?"

Jane sat still, her expression a mix of anger and embarrassment.

Already agitated, Bingley continued. "All my fault, is it? Miss Elizabeth asked Mrs Bennet to modulate her voice or to quit saying such obscenely stupid things. Did you know that? I heard it from Louisa who overheard it directly."

Jane blushed in mortification. Through all the discussions they had, she had not quite understood how badly her mother had acted at that infernal ball. She had thought herself in the throes of young love and that all the world's problems could be solved by love alone.

How stupid I have been.

Suddenly, Miss Bingley's shrill voice was heard. "We must not forget the wild behaviour of the younger Bennet sisters."

The fire in Jane was reignited. "Is it your assertion that you left me because of my mother's behaviour, which you did not witness, or my sisters' behaviour, which you did not witness? Mayhap you wish now to take my father to task, sir. These are heavy rebukes, heavy rebukes indeed."

Then Jane turned her attention directly on his sister. "Do not compare the behaviour of my sisters, mere girls, to that of you and Mrs Hurst, both well past childhood. The two of you spent every waking minute at Netherfield complaining about this and that and insulting your hosts and guests for their country manners, limited society, and dull gowns. Parading around in gowns and bonnets meant for the theatre looks ridiculous in the country."

"In town, too." The colonel smirked.

Miss Bingley caught the insult and replied sharply, "You call yourself a gentleman?"

"I cannot claim always to act like a gentleman, but I can assert that when I learn I have done wrong, I try to make amends. I cannot take all the credit, but Darcy and Elizabeth are very close to an engagement now because I—"

He could not continue because Miss Bingley let out a piercing scream.

The colonel waited for her to finish, then ignored the outburst entirely and continued as though it were insignificant. "As I was saying, I apologised, and I corrected my bad behaviour. I made amends. I did the gentlemanly thing. Time will tell whether it was adequate, but I did try my best. When have you tried your best—or even acknowledged wrongdoing?"

When Miss Bingley remained silent, Jane turned to Colonel Fitzwilliam. "You are too harsh on yourself. It is true that you and Darcy acted in ways that hurt us but never deliberately. He did it in service of a friend, and misguided or not, his motives were pure. When the two of you learnt of your errors, you *immediately* corrected them."

The colonel nodded his appreciation. Jane graced him with a smile and turned back to Miss Bingley.

"You, on the other hand, did everything by design. Within the hearing of servants we have known all our lives, you continually disparaged my family, apparently unaware just how badly you were behaving."

Mrs Hurst gasped.

"Oh, do not worry. The servants did not sully your reputation by repeating what you said until you were well quit of the neighbourhood, and they did not do so publicly. Nobody but Lizzy and I know, and we are not malicious gossips."

Bingley rubbed his face. "Thank you for that, Miss Bennet."

"I am not angry with you, sir. For months, I was hurt and despondent over you from your actions and neglect, but I am quite over that now. With your sisters, I feel I cannot think of anything I can do to make your situation more pitiable than it is or any way to punish you any worse than you are voluntarily punishing yourself right now."

Belatedly and stupidly gaining a bit of backbone, Bingley scowled. "On the contrary, Miss Bennet. Perhaps I narrowly escaped."

Jane let out a short laugh. "Perhaps you did, sir. I shall admit my family may not be the most decorous, but they are not bad enough to dissuade Fitzwilliam Darcy."

Jane looked at the colonel. "Your turn, Richard."

He was enjoying the show so much he almost forgot the message he was to deliver, but he was trained to follow orders.

"I have one message for you from Darcy, the Bennets, and myself —and you can assume the rest of my family as well. It is likely you will see us occasionally in company."

He turned towards the sisters. "Miss Bingley and Mrs Hurst, you will avoid all of us assiduously, and that includes Darcy. You may no longer use Darcy's name to gain admittance to society events. If you encounter us, avoid being within a dozen yards and ignore us entirely. If you completely ignore us, we shall ignore you."

He stood up straighter and stared hard at Miss Bingley, making sure she was listening. "But make no mistake. If you approach us, greet us, or say anything within our hearing indicating any connexion whatsoever, we shall give you the cut direct. By saying 'we,' I include my mother, Lady Matlock."

The colonel turned to an ashen-faced Bingley. "I shall not speak for Darcy, but I suspect he feels guilty about giving you bad advice. He did not tell you to have your sister write a letter indicating Georgiana had formed an attachment with you. He did not tell you to slink out in the middle of the night. I suspect he might want to retain your friendship, but only after you get your house in order and your dependents under better regulation.

"Finally, rumours are a terrible thing, but you should remember that most can be traced back to their source, given sufficient time and energy. Lady Matlock has both, and she takes our family name seriously. Do not start rumours or repeat them. Whatever you know, or think you know, or are told—keep it to yourself."

With that, Colonel Fitzwilliam gestured to the door with the clear implication that they were done, and there was nothing more to say. He allowed Bingley to escort his sisters or not as he chose. They were to leave and never return, and that was good enough for him.

After Georgiana took Mr Gardiner's arm, the colonel offered his own to Jane. He had to admit that she was fierce when she wanted to be, and that was not a terrible attribute for a woman—not terrible at all.

CHAPTER TWENTY-ONE

•●————————————●•

Worth Fighting For

THE TRIP DOWN THE STAIRS, THROUGH THE HALLS, DOWN THE stairs, across the corridors, down the stairs, and through the halls to the front door was not quite as tense as one would expect—at least for some in the party.

Jane spent the time speaking quietly with the colonel and found he had a wicked wit that reminded her very much of Elizabeth. She reflected that at one time, Elizabeth probably thought the colonel an amiable man who might have made a good match if her situation had been better. At the time, Jane would have agreed.

Upon reflection, she felt differently. While she had not suddenly become more knowledgeable and worldly in the past weeks and months, Jane had managed to forsake some of her preconceptions. She had begun to think differently about the relations between a man and a woman. She recognised that to pair the colonel with Elizabeth would have been similar to what she might have experienced with Mr Bingley. Either pairing would offer an excess of similarity.

Between herself and Mr Bingley, there would be too much agreement, too much amiability, too much indecision. Of

course, that would also imply all the corollaries: too little resolution, too little backbone, too much indecision.

Elizabeth and the colonel also shared similar natures: too
much impertinence, too much cynicism, too much decisive-
ness, and all the opposite corollaries.

Her sister needed a man of a steady nature to smooth out
her rough edges, and ideally a man who needed her liveliness
to overcome his shyness. In the end, Elizabeth needed a man
who needed her! That meant their natures would need to be
complementary, rather than similar—a man very much like
Darcy.

The colonel, from what she had seen, was quite a lively
man who hid his darker feelings well. It seemed certain that a
soldier did not gain the rank of colonel without experiencing a
great deal of unpleasantness, even if his father was an earl.
The colonel did not need a lively woman. He needed a steady
woman, a nurturing woman, a woman who could give him a
bit of peace when he needed it and perhaps an occasional kick
for motivation.

Much as she disliked being the subject of her own matchmaking mama, Jane decided she would do her best to help the
colonel find a wife. The man obviously could not be left to his
own devices, since he was over thirty and had joked that he
had never been close enough to matrimony to be frightened.

As they approached the entrance door, Jane saw servants
bringing coats, bonnets, and gloves for the departing members
of the party. The Bingleys were preparing to take their leave,
when Mrs Hurst broke free to approach her.

"Miss Bennet, I regret it will make little difference now,
but I would like to apologise for my behaviour. I had no idea
what Caroline wrote to you, but I was a willing participant in
the rest of the scheme, and for that I am ashamed."

"Are you ashamed or simply aware that you and your sister have climbed far out on a limb that is perilously close to breaking?"

"I suppose we shall never know. At this point, my situation is so poor that doing the right thing and doing the practical thing are one and the same. My character is not really being tested at this moment, is it?"

Jane considered the matter. There had been a time when she would have forgiven the woman almost immediately at the slightest sign of contrition. She had recently begun to challenge that idea.

Would that be her strategy when her children were naughty? It seemed that approach would give her half a dozen Lydias. Was she to let her servants and the shopkeepers cheat her without qualms or fear of retribution? Certainly not! Where was the right balance? Jane thought she would have to find a husband with a bit of backbone to keep her from sliding into old habits.

"Never is a very long time, Mrs Hurst. I suppose if you want to test your character, you must expose it to more situations and pay attention to how often you do the selfish thing versus the right thing. I believe in redemption, so if over time you find yourself bending towards the right and away from the selfish, you will find your character improving."

The lady was deep in thought. Jane hazarded a glance at Miss Bingley and her brother, both red-faced and angry.

Mrs Hurst finally spoke. "Thank you, Miss Bennet. You have given me something to think about, something to strive for."

"You owe me nothing. I only reminded you of what you already knew."

"I suppose so," she said with just the slightest bit of optimism in her voice.

Jane hazarded an amendment. "You remind me of my sister Kitty. She emulates my youngest sister, Lydia, who is rather like a younger version of Miss Bingley. I always thought Kitty could become a far better person if we could get her to follow someone more admirable, or at the very least, separate her from Lydia's influence."

"Come along, Louisa. Our friends will be waiting."

The disparaging way Miss Bingley said our friends set Jane's teeth on edge, and she had another epiphany. Both Lydia and Miss Bingley needed an audience. The fact that others were willing to follow their lead and tolerate their nonsense was one of the core parts of their being. Were Kitty and Mrs Hurst wicked people, or were they simply weak?

Jane had to admit that four months prior, she had been a weak person herself. She had allowed her parents, the local society, her sisters, and her own insecurities to drive her behaviour. She had been ready to marry Mr Bingley when she knew hardly anything about him!

"I was much like you a few months ago, Mrs Hurst. May I offer a suggestion?"

"Most certainly!"

"Separate yourself and your husband from your siblings. Not only by a few houses but by a few counties. Not for weeks, but for months or years. Put yourself out of your sister's reach, and strive to make your own life. You will be attached to your husband for the rest of your lives. Do you truly want another fifty years like the last one?"

The colonel surprised Jane by adding, "No time like the present, Mrs Hurst. If you like, I shall see you delivered to your husband. My aunt has several carriages and will loan me one if I ask nicely."

The lady said, "How do you know I am just weak and not vicious?"

"Because people are not condemned to be what they are forever, madam. I have seen soldiers I wanted to shoot myself who later turned out to be the best of men."

She looked sceptical, so the colonel stepped closer and spoke softly. "Character is worth fighting for, Mrs Hurst. It all depends on whether you are willing to fight or not. You cannot win without effort."

"I shall accept your generous offer, Colonel. I shall tell my brother I shall not take his coach. I like the idea of a total separation. I cannot promise a complete reformation, but I shall try."

"That is all anyone can ask, Mrs Hurst."

Within five minutes, Mr and Miss Bingley had left in their carriage, the colonel had ordered one of Lady Catherine's coaches as though he owned Rosings, and over the vigorous objections of her sister, Mrs Hurst was on her way, accompanied by her maid.

That settled, the party decided to return to the main parlour and see how that conversation had gone.

"Lady Catherine and her guests have moved to the yellow parlour, Colonel," Greaves told them.

While the colonel looked poleaxed by the news, Greaves discreetly winked at Jane which set her to giggling.

"Pray, what is so frightening about the yellow parlour?"

"You will see. Shall we?" the colonel said, before leading the group down the hall to a nondescript door.

The surprise was evident when they entered. They found themselves in a room that could only be described as intimate.

The small room was decorated in muted pastel colours of which yellow was predominant but certainly not overwhelming. Four sofas were arranged in a square around a small table. To Jane, it resembled a repurposed nursery and only lacked pictures of animals, rocking chairs, and cradles.

Lady Catherine and Miss de Bourgh were seated on one of the sofas to the left, the mother looking surprisingly calm, and her daughter surprisingly excited.

How could Elizabeth have described Darcy's cousin as pale and sickly? While it was true that she in no way could be considered robust, Jane thought there was certainly nothing wrong in her appearance or her smile that day.

On another sofa, Elizabeth and Darcy sat at an appropriate distance, but they shared looks that seemed as intimate as though she were sitting on his lap. It seemed clear to Jane that some dam had broken loose in Elizabeth, and her gaze towards her soon-to-be-intended had somehow lost all traces of ambiguity—at least to Jane's discerning eye.

She had felt for some time that Elizabeth cared for a man who had at long last admitted he knew what it was to love, and now it would appear she had joined him in that happy state.

CHAPTER TWENTY-TWO

The New Plan

AFTER THE NEWCOMERS HAD TAKEN SEATS ON THE TWO remaining sofas, Darcy watched as Anne fairly bounced in her seat.

"Welcome! Welcome!" she cried, looking at Jane and Mr Gardiner.

"Anne, how am I expected to teach Mrs Bennet and her two youngest decorum if I have been teaching you for the better part of two decades, and this is the best you can do?" Lady Catherine replied in a tone that sounded more teasing than censorious.

Anne laughed gaily. "We are to be cousins, Mama. I am just saving a few steps."

Jane turned to Lady Catherine. "I realise our introduction was somewhat unorthodox and incomplete, my lady, but may I say I am happy to meet you. Lizzy has said much about you, and I have been anxious to make your acquaintance."

Lady Catherine surprised Darcy by asking, "Have the vermin been cleared out?"

"If you mean did Gardiner and I just enjoy a quiet half an

hour of sport watching Georgie and Jane take them apart, then yes. All is as it should be."

The colonel laughed and turned to his cousin. "I think Miss Bingley is irredeemable, but Bingley seems as though he just needs to grow up. Perhaps you could loan him some pride."

Elizabeth smiled and said, "You can certainly spare it."

Darcy rolled his eyes, happy to be teased. "I have been trying to help him for a while, but at least recently, I believe I have been more of a hindrance than a help. I shall wait for the dust to settle and then see whether there is anything to salvage."

They were interrupted by Greaves bringing tea and sandwiches, since those who had gone to the grey parlour had not enjoyed any refreshment.

Once the servant left, Jane asked, "Lizzy, I gather from Lady Catherine's remark that she has agreed to take up the yoke."

"Yes, and I am very appreciative."

Darcy took a long sip of tea to hide a smirk. He thought having his aunt teach Mrs Bennet decorum was like asking a cow to teach a fish to fly, but he was not overly concerned. He assumed Elizabeth knew what she was about, and it was one less thing to worry him.

It took a quarter of an hour to tell what each group had done, and everyone remarked they were sad they had missed half of the events. The Bingleys were taken care of, the family at Rosings was taken care of, and all was right with the world.

After they had eaten, Anne said, "Lizzy, may I ask you an impertinent question?"

"Is any other kind allowed at Rosings?"

Anne became serious. "Is there any chance Darcy's suit will not succeed?"

The question was startling, both in its complete lack of propriety and its deeply personal nature. Darcy looked at Elizabeth to see how she would react. He was happy to see she did not take offence but seemed to be pondering the question deeply.

She finally looked at him with a gentle expression and smiled. "No."

The confirmation made him feel as though he were floating on air, but Elizabeth was not finished.

She spoke to the group. "I presume you all know what an avalanche is?"

She looked into Darcy's eyes. "That is how my feelings have been progressing. Your apology was like the first rock being knocked off a mountain, and it started rolling down, knocking snow loose as it fell. Our conversations and other efforts helped it gain momentum, gather more force, and at this moment, I am completely in love with you. If you happened to have a special licence in your pocket, I would have no qualms about walking over to the chapel and coercing my cousin to marry us right now."

Darcy's smile lit the whole room, and he reached into his waistcoat as though he had the licence, making everyone laugh gaily.

"It seems this is the one time in my life I failed to make an arrogant presumption."

Elizabeth smiled up at him.

"Good," said Anne. Her loud exclamation briefly drew attention away from Darcy and Elizabeth. "I hate to change the subject, but now that we are all here, I would like to discuss my disposition."

Darcy awakened from the haze of love and longing that clouded his mind. He looked at his cousin with new eyes and wondered what her life had been like. They had long ago determined they would never marry, and he had offered to do anything he could for her comfort, but otherwise, they had not had a lot to say to each other over the last several years. If they were not related, they would have been indifferent acquaintances at best.

Elizabeth asked gently, "What do you have in mind, Anne?"

"For many years now, you have been offering to help me, Darcy. You offered to take me away from Rosings for a week or a year if I wished it. You have offered me more and better books, more and better doctors, trips to town or the seaside, and everything else you could think of. You have done the same, Richard.

"Your offers were admirable and made me respect both of you. I should have told you this sooner, but they were all based on a false premise."

"What premise, Anne?" Jane asked.

"Do you know what is wrong with my life?"

Darcy saw everyone shaking their heads in confusion or ignorance.

Anne smiled at her mother. "*Nothing*! Not a thing. All your offers are solutions in search of a problem. I am perfectly happy. I am content."

Darcy and Richard exchanged surprised looks while Anne went on to explain.

"I have my books. Mrs Jenkinson and I get on very well. I have my phaeton and the gardens of Rosings. I can eat whatever I want whenever I want. I am rich enough to buy any trinket I desire or travel anywhere I wish to go. In fact, I have more money than I could possibly spend. I am not expected by a single person in the world to live a long life, but I shall live a good life. I am probably the most *content* person in this room."

Mr Gardiner recovered from his shock first. "What about marriage, Miss de Bourgh? Children?"

Anne shook her head. "I always considered children to be noisy, smelly, unpleasant things."

Mr Gardiner chuckled. "Some would say the same about husbands."

Darcy grew more serious. "Just to be clear. You do not wish to marry...ever?"

Anne smiled serenely. "No, I do not. Even if I did, I strongly suspect childbirth would kill me. I am not likely to survive to a ripe old age, regardless of what I do. Mama will probably outlive me, and aside from the pain that will cause her, I am content as can be."

Darcy looked at Lady Catherine, relieved to see she was not distraught by her daughter's mordant announcement, before returning his attention to Anne.

"That was not your primary point, I assume?"

"Oh no! It is but the preamble, Cousin. I want you to explain the implications of what I plan to do."

"Why me?" Darcy asked somewhat petulantly. He had never been as easy as he was at this moment, sitting closely and comfortably with Elizabeth, and he would much rather enjoy the feeling for a few more minutes.

"Moral authority, Cousin. Everyone will believe it coming from you."

He was still confused because the idea that someone would not want to marry had never occurred to him. Regardless of how much men grumbled about the 'parson's mousetrap', any man of sense wanted to be married.

He shifted into a posture more conducive to intelligent thinking. Finally, Darcy said, "I suppose the obvious problem is one of inheritance."

"Yes, the issue becomes somewhat murky," Lady Catherine said.

"Not at all. You have just not thought it through, Mother. Let me ask you a simple question. Why do first sons inherit and leave second and third sons to shift for themselves in the church, law, or military? Why do daughters get dowries? What is the purpose for entails?"

Elizabeth asked, "Are these all related?"

"Yes, of course."

"Setting aside any discussion of the peerage, it is to keep money and power in families, and I suppose, in *prominent* families, to give continuity to the estate's dependents, although many in our class disregard that aspect," Darcy offered.

Anne asked, "And is it just and natural to do so?"

Darcy thought carefully for a minute. "Since I am the recipient of both the status and the responsibility, I am a poor judge. My bias will be obvious."

"Perhaps I can be more objective," the colonel said. "While I am not entirely convinced it is just, you do have to admit it is efficient. Every society we know works the same. Whether it is just or natural, in England, it at least works. As the less fortunate second son, I can say it stings a bit for the individual, but it works for the family."

"I own I am intrigued," Mr Gardiner said. "I suppose if every generation of Fitzwilliams split their wealth among all of the sons, it would never have amassed enough power to amount to anything. You may lament not being the first son, but you are the second son of an earl. I believe it is much better to be a daughter or second son of a prosperous and important family than the first son of one that is diminished."

"This all seems obvious. It is just the way things are," Lady Catherine said. "Few of us think on it any more than we think about why horses are used to move carriages."

Anne continued. "We have established the first part of my thesis. Darcy, what is my present position *vis-à-vis* inheritance?"

"You are the heir apparent."

"Forgive me, but what exactly does that mean?" Jane enquired.

Darcy saw she was embarrassed to ask such a basic question. "There are two types of heirs. The heir apparent is the heir who cannot be displaced—typically, the eldest son. The heir presumptive is only the heir if no heir apparent can be found, and he could be supplanted. He is basically second in the line of succession.

"For example, Mr Collins is the heir presumptive to Longbourn, but if your mother were to have a son, or should she die and your father remarry and have a son with his new wife, that son would become the heir apparent, displacing Mr Collins."

Elizabeth laughed uneasily. "Well, that idea is disturbing, but it makes sense."

Anne said, "You are close, Darcy. Have you worked it out yet?"

Darcy was thoughtful for a moment. "I see where you are going, and I do not know what I think of the idea."

Lady Catherine said, "I do not."

Darcy looked to Elizabeth. "Would you care to comment?"

"It is all becoming clear now." Elizabeth turned to Anne. "What do you think of the heir presumptive?"

Anne smiled, "Simon de Bourgh is my cousin. I think very highly of him."

Elizabeth said, "Then it all makes sense."

"Perhaps to *you*," Jane said.

Darcy said. "Anne's point is that we are all looking at this wrong, at least according to the usual traditions. Anne will inherit Rosings at the age specified by her father's will. Lady Catherine has a life tenancy, much like Mr. Bennet, and the estate is held in trust.   If she marries, it belongs to her husband. If I married Anne, Rosings would serve to raise the status and importance of the *Darcy* family. It would be the same for any other suitor. Anne is suggesting it would be more just to keep it in the *de Bourgh* family, particularly if she does not wish to marry."

Jane still looked confused, so Darcy said, "Anne asked for the full description of the heir apparent. They are the heir unless they die or are disinherited."

Jane gasped and looked at Anne who smiled brightly.

"Yes! I want to be disinherited."

Lady Catherine cried, "You are insane, Anne!"

Anne looked at her contritely. "Mama, sometimes I think you believe you are still a Fitzwilliam. Your connexion to Lady Anne kept you close to the Darcys, but I think you have occasionally forgotten that you are a de Bourgh. You married my father by your own choice from a vast collection of potential suitors. You have had a good life…an important life…a well-lived life as mistress of this estate. I would happily see you mistress for life, or until you tire of the job, but the estate should by all rights go back to the de Bourgh family on your death. If the positions were reversed, you would be arguing that case at the top of your lungs."

Despite her apparent desire to rail against the argument, Lady Catherine said grudgingly, "I suppose there is some logic in that. If—and I do mean *if*—I find the man suitable, I suppose I could be persuaded, though I really have no control in the end. The ultimate decision is yours. Even excepting Rosings, you have a great fortune. The way you live, it would keep you in comfort forever. Yes, I suppose it might work. Simon would have to move in and start learning how to manage the estate, and I would move to the dower house, but it could be done."

Anne smiled. "That was far easier than I thought it would be."

Lady Catherine looked the most motherly Darcy had ever seen her.

"You know I would do anything for you," she said. "I assume you would want Darcy to remain as your trustee and confidante to ensure your needs are met."

"Of course." She glanced at Elizabeth. "I should like to live at Pemberley part of the time if Lizzy allows it."

"You would be most welcome at any time, Anne."

Darcy was quite surprised by Anne's sudden defection from the ranks of heiresses but had to admit that it made sense. Anne was Lewis de Bourgh's heir, she was of age, and of sound mind. Rosings was his legacy, so she could do with it as she pleased. If she wanted to keep it in the de Bourgh line, it was her right and privilege. He had long thought she should take control of her own life.

As the day had been long and conversations rather fevered, everyone left to take an hour or so to refresh themselves before dinner.

CHAPTER TWENTY-THREE

The Felicity Schedule

DARCY WALKED INTO THE SALOON HALF AN HOUR BEFORE dinner and bowed to the gentleman he found there. "Quite a day, eh, Gardiner?"

His companion laughed. "Yes, my friend, quite a day at that."

"Brandy?"

"It seems unlikely to harm us."

Darcy poured two tumblers. It was not the best brandy he had ever had, nor was it the second or third best, but it was adequate for his purpose.

"It is good to have a moment alone, Darcy. I wanted to speak to you."

"I am at your disposal, sir."

Darcy was fond of the older gentleman. Mr Gardiner was younger than Mr Bennet but old enough to have had significant life experience. Considering he had married Mrs Gardiner, he was obviously a more sensible man than Mr Bennet, and no censure could be made about how the gentleman conducted his business and his life. Darcy was quite happy to have the man's acquaintance, and he thought he might have appreciated him even if Mr Gardiner did not come with quite such an enchanting niece.

The two men walked over to a pair of chairs in the far corner.

For Darcy's part, he had been surprised at his aunt's rapid capitulation. He was under no illusion that she had done so for him. He was of the firmest opinion that it was all his Elizabeth's doing, although he would be hard-pressed to say exactly how she accomplished the task.

When they were seated, Mr Gardiner said, "I wanted to discuss your courtship of Elizabeth—more specifically, my insistence on a period of at least two months' duration before a proposal."

Darcy gave him a thoughtful look. "There is no need for concern, sir. Elizabeth and I discussed it, and we are quite in agreement. In fact, at her request, we decided to keep to exactly two months. I have promised to ask for her hand on the thirteenth of June."

Gardiner took another slow sip. "That is all well and good, but I do know what it is like to be young, in love, and somewhat frustrated. Earlier in the day, I believe I could have lit a cigar quite easily by simply holding it between the two of you."

Darcy reddened and stared at his boots. "I am a gentleman, and I shall act accordingly. The last thing in the world I want to do is make you or Mrs Gardiner uncomfortable. You have been very supportive of my suit and our understanding. I appreciate it immensely, and I am certain Elizabeth does as well, although you, of all people, know the folly of speaking for her."

"That is folly for any woman, sir, but a greater folly for some than others."

Darcy's mouth twitched. "I take your meaning."

Both men sipped their brandy in silence for a time until Mr Gardiner said, "Your courtship has been unusual. As Elizabeth has said, events have allowed your understanding to progress far faster than most courting couples and far faster than any of us expected. You started with a mighty deficit, but I believe you have come to know each other with startling speed."

"I shall not deny it has been exhilarating."

Mr Gardiner looked carefully at the young man he liked very much. He remembered when he was calling on Madeline Lewis. He was responsible for himself, his horse, and two clerks. Although he was about the same age as Darcy, and he started with almost nothing, there was essentially no price for mistakes. The worst that could happen was that he could bankrupt himself.

Darcy, on the other hand, had been responsible for hundreds of people. Even with some margin for error, every mistake would be costly to others. That would certainly weigh on a young man.

When he had been courting Madeline, he had little to offer, but there were no others vying for her hand or his. Conversely, Darcy had been hunted by ladies and their parents for over a decade. That would also have an effect, and the only surprise was that Darcy had not been made more reticent or arrogant by it.

"You are a grown man. Elizabeth is a grown woman," Gardiner finally said. "You have resolved your understanding and differences. I no longer feel any compulsion to coddle you, so I shall remove my restriction. You may ask the question at your convenience."

"What question is that, Uncle?" Elizabeth asked over his shoulder. She laughed when both men startled enough to spill their drinks.

"Lizzy, you know full well you should not sneak up on people."

"Let me rephrase that for you. I should know better than to walk into a public room with an open door and approach two men close to my heart, one of whom is champing at the bit for my company? Is that what you meant?"

Her look of innocence fooled nobody, but Gardiner conceded defeat gracefully with a chuckle.

Darcy joined in. "We were discussing proposals. Your uncle was suggesting I am an irresolute man, and we are a procrastinating couple because we follow directions."

Elizabeth smiled brightly. "I assume my uncle is tired of acting like a nursemaid and suggested we get on with it?"

Darcy looked up at her, smiled, and held out his hand. "More or less."

Elizabeth ran around the chair to face him and clapped her hands together. "Oh, I like proposals…or at least, well-done proposals."

Gardiner, feeling very much *de trop*, said, "These things are usually done privately. I shall take my leave."

"Oh, you need not worry, Uncle. All of our important conversations have been before witnesses."

"There will be aspects of our marriage that should be private, Elizabeth," Darcy said.

Gardiner stood up and moved swiftly away. The door clicked quietly behind him.

"Well-done proposals?" Darcy asked.

Elizabeth felt butterflies in her stomach but was not quite willing to abandon impertinence, mainly because this was such a momentous event.

"Yes! I suggest you refrain from mentioning your reasons for marrying, and we can definitely refrain from any mention of Lady Catherine."

"I think if I had proposed to you when I planned to, it would have been at best the second-worst proposal in history, and that would be optimistic."

She smiled shyly. "Yes, but I did not love you then. I suspect that makes things easier now."

"Do you have any other suggestions?"

She looked into his eyes. "Do not get on your knees as though you are begging. We shall each have our own area of expertise and responsibility, but in essentials, we are equals."

He smiled. "No knees—although I am not certain I can promise to avoid begging."

She giggled. It was an unconventional proposal, but nearly everything else between them had been so.

Darcy continued, "Have you anything else to propose for my domestic felicity?"

"No poetry! Absolutely no poetry!"

"Ah, but we have a fine, stout, healthy love. If I remember correctly, everything nourishes what is strong already. I suspect we could survive several sonnets."

"Yes, but why take chances?"

By that time, Darcy had abandoned his chair without even being aware of it, and they stood close, with less than an inch between them. He felt no need to check for privacy, assuming that Elizabeth's uncle was standing guard on the other side of the door.

Darcy felt his own nervousness, but it was tempered by a feeling of love and confidence in their *shared* future.

"On the subject of fine, stout, healthy loves," Darcy whispered softly, "Miss Elizabeth Bennet, you are the love and light of my life. Everything about our lives has improved since we met. You are the perfect mirror to my imperfect soul. Your modesty perfectly balances my pride. Your impertinence and wit overcome my reserve and conceit. My life is vastly improved with you in it. My love increases and our lives improve every day we are together. Would you do me the great honour of becoming my wife?"

"It would be my pleasure and my privilege, Fitzwilliam."

No further discussion was necessary before their lips came together softly and tenderly, with no pretence and no plan.

The first kiss was shy, slow, and tentative, but it was not long until her hands left his so she could wrap her arms about his neck, and his arms went around her waist. Darcy deepened the kiss, feeling the contradiction between the desire to extend the moment until the end of time and wanting to do everything and feel everything immediately. He could not describe the feelings of love that formed in his breast, surmising they could not be explained to anyone who had not experienced them, and there would be little point explaining to someone who had.

Darcy had no idea how long the kiss went on. In one sense, he felt as though he could carry her off to his chambers immediately, but in another, he felt that if their courtship dragged out for a month, they should savour every incremental increase in intimacy. The contradiction did not bother him in the least. They would have decades to sort it out.

Eventually, after many multiples of what would have been considered proper, they pulled apart.

Darcy asked, "Are you happy, my love?"

Unable to respond in words, Elizabeth pulled his head down to hers and kissed him again. When she broke the kiss, she touched her forehead to his and whispered softly, "Short engagement?"

He chuckled. "I truly wish I had bought a licence, but I do need to speak to your father, and I suppose we need to give your mother her due."

Elizabeth laughed openly. "She was right, you know."

"How so?"

"Sending Jane to Netherfield riding a horse in the rain was the ideal strategy for catching a rich husband."

They laughed light-heartedly, and Darcy decided that if Lady Catherine could be brought to his side, then Mrs Bennet should be easy by comparison. Regardless of what else happened, Elizabeth's mother's machinations had set his destiny in place. He had to admit that without the sight of Elizabeth after walking three miles, the skirts above her ankles covered in mud, and with her fine eyes brightened by the exercise, he would never have been as happy as he was at that moment.

Feeling that betrothals should ideally be measured in hours, but knowing they would have to settle for weeks, the couple finally walked across the saloon and opened the door to find all their friends and family ready to greet them. Elizabeth was quite happy that they did not all tumble into the room, as they had when Mr Collins proposed, so she thought her family's manners had already improved.

"Well?" Lady Catherine said eagerly.

"It is done," Darcy replied with a grin, leaving no one the least bit confused about what it was.

Even though he was Elizabeth's closest relative, Mr Gardiner stepped back slightly, giving Lady Catherine the privilege of being the first to congratulate the newly engaged couple.

"It is hard to believe, considering how dour you were before, Darcy, but I think you are to be the happiest couple in the world. While others smile, you will laugh. My congratulations. You have worked quite some magic, Elizabeth, and I shall be happy to call you niece."

Elizabeth reached out to the grand dame and gave her a hug. It was returned quite stiffly, since the lady had probably not done anything like that in a very long time, but their embrace ended with tears in both women's eyes.

Anne seemed about ready to burst with joy. Elizabeth was suspicious about Anne's assertion that there was nothing to be improved in her life, but fortunately, she thought it would not require any intervention on her part. The young soon-to-be-former heiress seemed lighter and happier than Elizabeth had ever seen her—although to be fair, anything short of unrelenting misery would seem an improvement. If Anne wanted more happiness in her life, she seemed to understand she only need strive for it.

After Darcy had released Georgiana from an embrace, it was Elizabeth's turn. She then worked her way to embrace Uncle Gardiner and Jane, chattering happily about her felicity, while the colonel gave Darcy a handshake and a manly slap on the back.

"You will be next, Cousin. If not this year, then perhaps next."

The colonel did not reply with his usual jest. If it was odd, only Elizabeth noticed it, just as she saw his gaze drift towards her sister as it had many times that evening.

Of course, Elizabeth's attention was better occupied. She and Darcy tried their best to talk to other people at dinner rather than to each other, but as expected, their best was not very good.

Everybody thought they would need a crowbar to pry the two apart, but when Lady Catherine called for the traditional separation of the sexes, they went without complaint. They knew they had their whole lives to spend together. As it was, they barely managed a distracted half an hour apart before the entire group moved to the drawing room and spent the rest of the evening listening to duets played by Elizabeth and Georgiana, with Jane occasionally adding her voice to the song.

It was magical.

CHAPTER TWENTY-FOUR

Going Home

NOBODY VOICED ANY COMPLAINTS ABOUT THE BREAKFAST AT Rosings. In fact, Mr Gardiner and Lady Catherine engaged in a detailed discussion about the sausage they were eating, including its provenance, ageing, spice mix, where the pigs were raised, and other factors that allowed the rest of the guests to ignore them. It appeared that, in Mr Gardiner, Lady Catherine had met her match, since he did not allow a single detail to go unchallenged.

Elizabeth and Darcy sat next to each other, much closer than propriety allowed. Jane and the colonel sat beside the happy couple, speaking easily about travelling and staying home. Georgiana and Anne sat opposite, deep in discussion about London fashions.

Finally taking a break from the discussion of sausage, Lady Catherine cleared her throat for attention.

"I have written to Simon de Bourgh. I gave hints that we had family business to discuss but nothing beyond that. I asked him to make plans to attend me three months hence for an extended stay, as I would like Darcy safely married, so my nephews and brother can attend. Simon will not think it unusual, as he has had similar visits before."

"I am looking forward to renewing our acquaintance, Mama," Anne said, "and I do so hope my cousins will join us." She gazed at Darcy and Elizabeth.

"I believe I shall be able to spare Fitzwilliam by then," Elizabeth said. "In fact, I intend to take advantage of the fixed schedule to force a short engagement, and I shall be anxious to spend more time with Mrs Collins."

Anne asked, "How short an engagement? Nothing unseemly, I hope?"

Darcy looked curiously at Elizabeth, who blithely said, "My father's permission will take half an hour of teasing followed by rapid capitulation. I shall be surprised if the wedding contract is not already drawn up. We can call the banns on Sunday and marry in a month without raising any eyebrows—aside from my mother's, of course."

Everyone agreed to the suitability of the plan, and the four young ladies began a lively discussion about weddings.

Greaves entered and whispered to Lady Catherine. She nodded to the butler, who turned to address the room.

"Mr Bingley asks if he might be allowed to address all assembled."

Everyone at the table exchanged looks, but Jane was the first to speak. "Is that all?"

With the typical butler's expressionless face, Greaves said drolly, "I omitted the numerous and lengthy apologies for the sake of brevity, Miss Bennet."

Amid the laughter, Lady Catherine turned to Jane, who indicated she had no objection to hearing what Mr Bingley had to say. Then she asked Darcy, "I presume you wish to keep your friendship with the gentleman?"

"I do, and I am the last man in the world with a right to criticise him for inconstancy."

Lady Catherine nodded at Greaves and the butler disappeared through the door. A moment later, Bingley came in looking contrite. He bowed to everyone at the table.

"My lady, I apologise for interrupting your breakfast, but I have some things I should like to say to everyone here—with your permission, of course. I regret I could not work out a more polite way to go about it."

He was obviously nervous, as the whole speech had come out so fast that he sounded like a chattering magpie.

Some sympathetic sense must have overcome Lady Catherine, for she gestured to him to fill his plate and sit down at the table. Bingley moved with alacrity and took a chair far away from Jane.

A quarter of an hour later, the group reconvened in the drawing room. Once everyone was seated, Lady Catherine looked at Mr Bingley.

"You may proceed."

He took a deep breath. "I have several things to say, starting with you, Miss Bennet, to whom I offer profound and sincere apologies. I treated you infamously last winter, and I offer no excuses. I cannot mitigate whatever heartache and discomfort you felt, nor do I particularly expect forgiveness. If I wish to be a gentleman, I should start acting like one and take responsibility for my own lack of resolve."

"Mr Bingley, I shall offer forgiveness. Whether you deserve it or not is irrelevant, as forgiveness is as much for the forgiver as for the transgressor. I am no longer willing to carry the burden of anger or despondency, and years hence, I suspect we may both feel it was all for the best."

Bingley wore a somewhat hang-dog expression. "I thank

you. I find it unlikely I shall ever feel it was for the best, but I shall try to believe it."

"Is not faith a key element of life, sir? Would we not live a miserable existence if we thought the world entirely capricious?"

Anne intervened. "Take the word of someone who has suffered considerably more than any of you aside from my mother. Faith in the future is the only thing that can pull you from melancholy. If you believe things will get worse, they generally do."

"I thank you for the advice, Miss de Bourgh. I shall do my best to live by it."

"You are young, Mr Bingley," Mr Gardiner said. "Young people frequently make stupid mistakes. I cannot count the number I made at your age. You have time to learn from your mistakes."

Bingley nodded gratefully to the older man.

"All of this is good advice," Jane added. "Having faith in a better outcome is necessary but insufficient. If you want to become a gentleman, Mr Bingley, you have other things to do. My pardon comes with some advice."

"Pray continue, Miss Bennet."

"How many of your Netherfield tenants have buildings that need repair? Are any of them sick or in need of assistance? Have you balanced and verified your steward's ledgers? Are there any disputes your steward could not solve? Did your sister discharge servants without reference, notice, adequate pay, or sufficient reason? Were your bills in Meryton paid on time? Need I continue?"

Bingley sheepishly shook his head.

"If you would become a gentleman, Mr Darcy should be your

model. If his manners are sometimes imperfect, he rectifies the matter as soon as he can, regardless of how difficult it might be. He never shirks his duty, even when it is unpleasant or difficult."

"That is good advice, madam, and I shall do my best to follow it." For a moment, Mr Bingley looked as though he might say more, but refrained in the end.

Jane graciously replied, "We all make mistakes, sir."

Bingley turned towards his friend. "That brings me to my second apology. Darcy, I apologise for putting you in the unenviable position of making all my decisions for me. You tried to teach me at Cambridge and at Netherfield, but in the end, I deferred to you on almost everything, including subjects upon which you had no business expressing strong opinions. It is entirely my fault that you established that habit, and so I offer an apology for it."

Darcy wore a pained expression. "We both have our share of the blame, Bingley. I accept your apology and offer mine for officious interference."

Elizabeth smirked. "We could go on all day, but I believe you have resolved the bulk of the issues. Someday, Mr Bingley, you will need more advice. At the very least, you will probably need a repetition of the things my intended has already told you, since you have given them insufficient attention. Shall we assume that the two of you can work that out in the proper way?"

Bingley smiled in almost his old jovial manner. "Your intended! That is wonderful news. I would have hoped for that outcome, but I must admit that when we left Netherfield, you appeared to hate the sight of each other."

Elizabeth laughed. "You were half right." She and Darcy exchanged a private look before she continued. "If you want to become a true gentleman, Mr Bingley, need I state the obvious?"

"I assume you mean in regard to my sister," he said with a sigh.

"Yes. You must make some decisions. You are not her father, but you have been placed in the position of acting as one. You must get her under control—or better yet—simply release her from your household, and let her shift for herself. She needs to develop independence."

"Setting her up in her own establishment would ruin her reputation," protested Bingley. "She would be considered on the shelf."

Jane stifled a laugh. "If Miss Bingley's reputation is in danger, it is her own doing. She is a handsome woman with a large dowry. If she quit reaching for that which she will never have, she could find a match in months."

With an arch look, Elizabeth said, "Your sister is a grown woman, so she should take responsibility for herself. The two of you," she added, looking at Bingley and Darcy, "allowed her to abuse Jane and me at Netherfield either by agreeing with her or ignoring her. I can assure you that such behaviour will not be allowed in my home in the future. One lifetime of it is quite enough."

Jane added her voice. "You should look at Longbourn for what your life will be like in a few years, Mr Bingley. My mother has some slight justification for her matchmaking, as the entail does put us in grave danger of genteel poverty, but she herself has made no attempt to economise. For years, she has thrown us at any man with an income, worried more for her own future comfort than ours.

"My father, on the other hand, has the education and experience to make a genteel household, but he does not trouble himself. Grasping and indolent, you and your sister are our parents twenty years ago. If you want to see your future, look no farther than Longbourn."

Bingley looked thoughtful. "I thank you for the advice, and I shall take some action. I suspect after yesterday, Caroline will be desperate to get away from me, so the problem may solve itself."

"That may be the case, but that does not absolve you of working on your own character," Elizabeth said.

"No, it does not." Mr Bingley stood. "I do not wish to take up your whole day. I just wanted to say one more thing." He looked at Darcy. "If you are going to Hertfordshire, I would like to put Netherfield at your disposal. You may consider the house as your own during your engagement."

Before Darcy could answer, Jane spoke up. "No, that will not do. It is your leased estate, Mr Bingley. It is your responsibility. It can survive without you, as it did for the two years it sat empty before you came, but if you quit at your first challenge, it will be all too easy to give up and return to a life of idleness. You must finish what you started. Your reception cannot possibly be any frostier than Darcy's will be, and you can see he is running into the flames, not out."

Looking stunned, Bingley sank back into his chair. "I would not want to impose on you. I could not entertain without a hostess in any case."

Suddenly Lady Catherine reminded everyone she was still in the room. "I shall be there. In fact, it seems convenient. I am not completely unversed in estate management or acting as mistress of an estate, Mr Bingley. Darcy will be fighting his own battles at Longbourn, but I have no qualms about advising you and serving as your hostess."

If that offer was intended to calm him, it had the opposite

effect. Bingley stuttered and stared a bit, but the impasse was broken by Mr Gardiner.

"What say you, Bingley? Shall we see what you are made of?"

Mr Bingley's gaze found Darcy's, and he nodded in agreement. "I happily accept your gracious offer, Lady Catherine."

CHAPTER TWENTY-FIVE

Fifty Miles

MR GARDINER HAD A PRESSING NEED TO RETURN TO HIS family and business, but he felt no real compunction about trusting his nieces for half a day to the care of two children of earls and the master of the largest estate in Derbyshire. That afternoon, he returned to London in the Darcy coach. If he briefly wished he could witness the hubbub that was about to ensue at Longbourn, he recovered from his disappointment by imagining his sister's voice upon hearing her least-favourite daughter was engaged to 'ten thousand a year'.

Everyone else left the following day after another hearty breakfast.

Mr Bingley had spent the night writing missives to his servants in London and Hertfordshire to prepare for their party's arrival. To ensure Netherfield's readiness, Lady Catherine sent several of her servants off early with the letters along with her own instructions.

Bingley took his coach and offered places to Anne and Georgiana. The rest rode in Lady Catherine's largest and most ornate coach and six. They traversed the fifty miles of good road in proper order. Much as Mr Collins had some months earlier, they arrived at four o'clock, albeit in better equipage.

Elizabeth imagined Kitty and Lydia were likely staring out the window wondering who could possibly arrive in such a fine carriage, which would naturally prompt Mrs Bennet into raptures about all the matrimonial wonders that must soon befall them. She and Jane thought their mother to be invariably silly but had to admit that even though most of her schemes were hare-brained and failure-prone, and many of her efforts caused more harm than good, in the end, she had fulfilled her hopes. Her daughter would indeed be married to one of the richest men in England. Of course, it was the wrong man, the wrong daughter, the wrong scheme, the wrong time, and the wrong circumstances—but still 'ten thousand a year and likely more'! Elizabeth leant her head against the squabs and smiled.

As the coach pulled into the drive at Longbourn, the place she had left less than two months earlier, Elizabeth realised she was no longer coming home. She had anticipated feeling some sort of strong emotion, both for her beloved Longbourn and her family, but in the end, she felt little more than impatience. She knew she would have to endure a month of aggravation before she could claim her rightful place with Darcy, but in her mind, she had already made the transition from daughter to wife. Elizabeth Bennet found that *home* was attached to the man sitting nervously beside her, regardless of where they happened to be.

When the footman placed the step, she took a deep breath, anticipating with no small amount of dread what sort of ridiculousness and folly were likely to follow.

It had been decided they would enter mostly by precedence, so Lady Catherine was followed by Darcy and Elizabeth, then the colonel and Jane, then Anne and Georgiana. Bingley went directly to Netherfield for obvious reasons.

Once inside, Elizabeth found her parents and sisters staring at their party in complete silence. Their confusion was obvious. Elizabeth was on the arm of Mr Darcy, her well-known sworn enemy, and Jane was on the arm of a gentleman in regimentals entirely unknown to them. Their daughters were in company with two unfamiliar ladies and a matron who looked as though she could easily take tea with the queen and criticise the pastries.

By design, Elizabeth stepped forward, her hand still firmly on Darcy's arm. "Lady Catherine de Bourgh, may I introduce my family. Mr Thomas Bennet, Mrs Fanny Bennet, and my sisters, Mary, Catherine, and Lydia."

"Mr Collins's esteemed patroness?" Lydia asked, wide-eyed.

She and Kitty both giggled but stopped as though slapped when Lady Catherine turned a frightening stare on them. The dowager nodded her head regally, while the family members gave bows and curtseys in something akin to proper deference.

Elizabeth reddened and completed the introductions, deliberately leaving Darcy until the end. "And of course, you all remember my intended, Mr Darcy."

Elizabeth found herself quite enjoying the stunned silence and confused expressions with which her family reacted to her news. Mr Bennet, for once, did not display a sardonic smirk. He looked amused but also quite puzzled, as though the world no longer made sense.

"*Intended? Intended!* Oh my! I always knew how it would be. I was sure you could not be..." Mrs Bennet's cries of joy sputtered as she finally worked out that it was not her most beautiful daughter who was engaged, and the prospective groom was not the ever-amiable Mr Bingley. Elizabeth smiled as her mother peered at her least-favourite daughter as though thinking, *How could you capture Mr Darcy?*

More out of habit than need, Mrs Bennet called for her salts. Jane began to step towards her mother but was stopped by a glance from Lady Catherine.

"Calm yourself, Mrs Bennet. I realise this is quite a shock, and in fact, I can sympathise with your plight. I must admit I was quite overcome by the news myself, but all will be well."

Elizabeth smiled up at Darcy, who gave her a warm look in return. She thought it all seemed to be going astonishingly well when Lydia finally overcame her shock.

"Lizzy married to dour Mr Darcy? What a good joke!"

Lady Catherine turned her head to glare at the upstart with a frown that could compete with a gorgon. Elizabeth was shocked to see Lydia cringe and abruptly stop laughing.

Hill entered the parlour, while Lady Catherine, acting in the only way she was constitutionally capable, took charge of the situation.

"I presume you are the housekeeper?"

"Yes, my lady," Hill said with complete composure. Anyone who had survived twenty years under Fanny Bennet's authority was not to be intimidated by the daughter of an earl.

"Are you a sensible woman?"

Elizabeth answered for her. "She is, indeed, Lady Catherine. She has often been the only voice of reason on the entire estate."

"Very well! We shall require tea for everyone except the two youngest. They are back to the schoolroom. They will not be out until they learn to act with the decorum expected of the sisters of my niece, the future Elizabeth Darcy."

As expected, Lydia let out a loud wail. "I shall do no such

thing. I am going to Meryton to visit the officers!" She began to walk out of the parlour with Kitty quickly following her.

Elizabeth watched as Lady Catherine eyed Mr Bennet to learn if he would take some action with his daughters, but when he remained smiling at the scene, she shook her head and asserted her authority.

"You have a choice to make, young ladies. I shall not allow you to bring ruin on my family, which you most assuredly will if you keep on in the wild manner to which you are accustomed."

When Lydia opened her mouth to protest, Lady Catherine's voice grew sharper. "Oh yes! I know it all from unimpeachable sources. At this point, your *choice* is the schoolroom or the nursery. *Decide now!*"

The sudden edge of iron in her voice at the last word finally stopped the girls.

"Papa, tell this horrid lady she cannot speak to us this way in our own home," Lydia whined.

For the briefest moment, Elizabeth hoped with all her might her father would recover from his indolence and take charge of his family. Alas, knowing him well for all her life— yet not really knowing him at all—she saw the instant when he accepted the course of action that would involve the least trouble and expense.

She could almost see the thought forming in his mind. *Well*, if Lizzy wants to take charge of my family, who am I to argue. While it could easily be said Elizabeth was not surprised, she was sorely disappointed.

Mrs Bennet had taken a seat, but remained blissfully silent, for which Elizabeth was eternally grateful.

She was further heartened when she heard Darcy's deep voice. "Mr Bennet, I believe we have things to discuss."

"I suppose we do, sir."

With a quick and chaste kiss to Elizabeth's fingers, Darcy followed the older man to his study.

Lydia and Kitty remained at the door.

Lady Catherine asked, "Do you seriously consider yourself up to a contest of wills with me?"

"Mama, tell her to leave me alone," Lydia whined, setting Elizabeth's teeth on edge.

Jane, who had seated herself with Mary, Anne, and Georgiana, had begun pouring tea. She looked up. "Colonel, did you bring the things I requested?"

"I did, Miss Bennet."

The distracting question threw everyone out of kilter, and the colonel stepped into the breach. He looked sternly at Kitty and Lydia.

"Lady Catherine has given you a choice. Since I am a true soldier, rather than one of the puffed-up dandies in the militia, and I am the son of an earl, will you take me at my word on some things?"

In the press and bustle, Lydia seemed to have forgotten there was a true redcoat in the room. In reply, she gave only an ill-mannered nod of her head.

Elizabeth was curious to learn what scheme Jane had devised, although from the expression worn by Lady Catherine, she suspected the dowager might be aware of the plan.

The colonel reached for the satchel he had carried into the parlour. He opened it, pulled out a leather pouch of coins, and tossed it on a small table.

"That, Miss Lydia, is the amount you spend each year. I am reliably informed that you have forty pounds, but your mother routinely supplements that for you and Miss Bennet. I am also told you frequently steal things from your sisters."

"I do not take—" Lydia started to scream but found herself unequal to the colonel's glare.

He next pulled out a length of rope and lobbed it on the table. "This is what thieves get in the regulars."

Kitty gasped, and Lydia gulped at the implication, which lacked any subtlety at all.

The colonel pulled out another leather pouch and threw it on the table. It was about half the size of the original. "That is what your actual pin money is, what your sisters live on."

Lydia had enough sense to stay quiet while the colonel removed another pouch about a quarter the size of the last one and threw it down. It made hardly a sound.

"This is what a lieutenant in the militia lives on once he pays for his board and such. Their wives have no servants at all. Their children are fed by the hand of their mothers or starve. If they are lucky, they *might* get one new dress a year."

Elizabeth was startled, and she could only wonder how her youngest, least worldly sisters would live in such a situation.

The colonel went on. "Of course, about one officer in ten is like Wickham, with whom you are familiar. From him, you would get a pleasing manner and promises, but no money at all, and no marriage or neat little house. Is that truly what you want?"

Lydia gulped, entirely silent for once.

"So, which is it to be, ladies. Schoolroom or nursery? Do you truly think yourselves equal to a battle of wills with Lady Catherine and me?" he said with a frightening growl.

The exhibition had been deliberately blunt. Elizabeth sought out Jane's attention and secured a nod that affirmed her eldest sister had approved such a stark warning.

"Schoolroom," whispered Lydia and Kitty in unison.

The colonel relented and said kindly, "You are both

young. It would take all day to list some of the stupid
things my cousin Darcy and I did as boys. However, you
are at the age where mistakes have consequences. The
job of your elders is to protect you from those. Take
heart, ladies. Your choices will be far better once you
have learnt a few lessons, and you have a new brother.
You will thank me for this little lecture in a year or
two."

Elizabeth saw that Lydia's scowl was hardly sufficient to
do anything other than make it difficult for the colonel to keep
from laughing.

"Your governess will be here in two days," Lady Catherine
said. "I shall be evaluating your education tomorrow. For the
moment, go and see to the comfort of the schoolroom. It must
be cleaned and organised."

Much to Elizabeth's surprise, the two sisters meekly left
the room and gave them some peace. Elizabeth looked to her
mother, who seemed to be in some shock and unwilling to
oppose Lady Catherine.

Darcy walked back into the room with a smile on his face,
the conference with Mr Bennet over surprisingly quickly. Elizabeth was undecided whether she was happy her father had
apparently refrained from extracting his share of amusement at
her intended's expense, or sad that he had quickly accepted
whatever settlement had been proposed. There was no doubt
the settlement would be far more generous than she could ever
have expected, but Elizabeth wished her father had shown
some interest and put some effort into ensuring her future
felicity.

Such maudlin thoughts could not survive the smile on
Darcy's face, and it took but a moment with his hand back in
hers for all to be right with the world.

She pressed his hand reassuringly and walked over to her mother.

"You are to have one daughter married—very well married! Our wedding is to be on the thirteenth of June. I know it is a surprise to all, but I love Mr Darcy very dearly. Can you be happy for me, Mama?"

Elizabeth could see the thoughts of carriages, pin money, dresses, and houses going through her mother's head, and she could just as well see the moment when the lady managed to quelch each thought. Elizabeth had no idea whether it was because Mrs Bennet was realising such contemplations would be unseemly to voice in front of Lady Catherine, she was intimidated by the company, or she just had nothing to say.

Mrs Bennet asked timidly, "You love him, Lizzy?"

"Yes, Mama. I do! He is the best man I have ever known, and I love him dearly."

"That is good. Who would have thought?" Then she looked at the man. "Mr Darcy, I do hope you will forgive me for having disliked you so intensely?"

Elizabeth took the question entirely in stride, knowing he would answer without taking offence.

"Your disapprobation was well-earned, Mrs Bennet. No forgiveness is necessary, and I do hope you will pardon my churlish manners when I was in the county."

"Oh pish!" she said, reclaiming a bit of her old vigour.

"He has apologised and made amends, Mama."

Elizabeth could see the strain her mother was under trying to keep the joy and advantages of the match to herself. She expected to hear a full hour or more of the benefits of having a daughter well married.

Much to Elizabeth's surprise, Georgiana and Anne had made the acquaintance of Mary while the rest of the drama was unfolding. She felt somewhat guilty that the traditionally ignored ladies had once again been overlooked, but she gave herself leave to repay any debt of attention later.

Elizabeth could tell she had interrupted a discussion of music between Georgiana and Mary, with Anne simply enjoying the conversation.

"Georgiana, there is a very good pianoforte at Netherfield. Mary will be your sister in a month. Perhaps you three could go and become better acquainted?"

The suggestion was twofold, and even though she had just thought of it, Elizabeth was gratified to see Darcy seemed to recognise the wisdom. They were to be relations soon. If they could not manage to acquaint and entertain themselves without Jane and Elizabeth's coddling, they had no hope of surviving in society.

Mary looked somewhat frightened at the suggestion, and Elizabeth could see Jane preparing to offer to smooth the way, but she dissuaded her with a subtle headshake. It was time for the younger siblings to stand on their own six feet.

She turned to Darcy. "You should return for supper."

He responded with a smile and quirked his eyebrow in a small signal she had learnt to mean that if nobody was here, he would have kissed her senseless.

Smiling, Elizabeth said, "Richard, you will come as well, of course."

The realisation that she was being even more dictatorial than Lady Catherine gave Elizabeth a brief pang, but it did not last long.

She winked at Lady Catherine. "I thank you for your able assistance, my lady, but I believe I must speak to my parents now."

"That seems wise, Elizabeth. I shall see what a jumble Mr Bingley has made of Netherfield."

Elizabeth had to laugh, forgetting her mother for a moment.

"Mr Bingley?" voiced Mrs Bennet.

Jane spoke up quickly and forthrightly. "Mama, Mr Bingley and I are indifferent acquaintances but nothing more, and I would beg you to take me at my word."

"But—" Mrs Bennet started.

"Mr Bingley is not a bad man, but he is not for me." Jane, for what Elizabeth believed might be the first time in her life, looked fiercely at her mother. "That is the last word on the subject to me or anybody else. Am I understood?"

In what Elizabeth considered a temporary victory at best, Mrs Bennet nodded in confused agreement.

With that, the three ladies of the house started everyone moving. Anne, Mary, and Georgiana had quit paying any attention to anyone else sometime earlier, and they were already in the front hall asking for their coats and bonnets before Darcy and the colonel even started to move.

Elizabeth waited until just the right moment to pull Darcy into a hidden alcove to give him a kiss that would almost certainly have brought on an apoplexy in a lesser man.

Fortunately, he survived and even managed to walk to the carriage in a straight line—mostly straight, at least.

CHAPTER TWENTY-SIX

Amalgamation

NOBODY COULD HAVE PREDICTED THE ODD COMBINATIONS OF personalities, quirks, and events that collided during the weeks of Elizabeth and Darcy's engagement.

The most poetic description for the first encounter came from Mary. She pronounced the visit behind closed doors between Mrs Bennet and Lady Catherine de Bourgh as akin to 'a gang of sailors watching a catfight in the middle of a badger den'. Elizabeth was prodigiously proud of both the cleverness of the analogy and Mary's bravery for sitting through the cacophony, albeit from a room away. The yelling and screeching coming from the parlour was prodigious, loud, and constant—for exactly one hour.

After that, both ladies exited as though nothing had happened, and they got on with the business of becoming fast friends. Elizabeth would have bet that neither lady was willing to cede the position of ultimate authority on a single issue— Lady Catherine because of her rank, experience at managing estates, and long-standing stubbornness and Mrs Bennet because it was, after all, *her* house and *her* daughter being married.

At the start of her engagement, Elizabeth had agreed to be paraded around the neighbourhood like a prize heifer, but she set strict limits. She gave her mother and Lady Catherine a schedule when she would be available and did whatever they asked during those few hours, with the understanding that if she was returned to Longbourn five minutes late, she would be absolved of the next day's visits.

Elizabeth resisted being placed in the awkward position between the women by simply ceding all authority for everything save the wedding dress and her trousseau to both ladies and vowing she would accept anything they agreed upon.

That plan worked well for the first week when she found herself in the first real discussion about the ceremony with her intended as they walked slowly up Oakham Mount.

"Fitzwilliam, do you have a strong opinion about the flowers at the chapel?"

"Do weddings usually have flowers?"

She laughed and swatted his chest. "Lady Catherine and Mama seem to have a disagreement they cannot resolve."

"How do you plan to resolve it?"

"You will see," she said with a smile, "I have a plan."

The flower issue came up the morning after her discussion with Darcy.

"You will have to make the decision, Lizzy. Lady Catherine and I cannot agree on the arrangement of flowers."

"I see. Should I presume you each wish to present your ideas so I can choose?"

"It seems only fair," Lady Catherine said, as though fairness had ever been a primary concern. "You are the bride, after all."

Elizabeth smiled. "Yes, I am the bride, so here is my decision. We shall have no flowers inside the chapel, just the traditional petals scattered on the path."

Both ladies looked like startled deer, while Darcy had to convert a guffaw into a poorly disguised cough.

Elizabeth continued. "To be honest, I have never cared much for flowers at weddings. I think it a silly tradition."

"No flowers?" both ladies bellowed in unison, apparently unaware that they sounded much closer to twins than two people of vastly different rank and fortune.

Elizabeth blithely turned to her intended. "Will your friends disparage you if there are no flowers?"

"To be honest, most of my friends are men, and the only thing that would change their attention to the ceremony would be if you replaced the flowers with stacks of wine bottles, cigars, or hunting dogs."

"There you have it! No need for flowers, and I believe we can abandon the idea of dogs as well." Elizabeth paused strategically before adding, "Unless you ladies can come to some accord."

Both agreed with alacrity, and that was the last decision about the ceremony Elizabeth made. There was no more contention until it came time to discuss her dress and trousseau. The discussion arose at breakfast, which Darcy and Colonel Fitzwilliam routinely took at Longbourn during the engagement.

"As much as I appreciate all you are doing, and while I would not dream of faulting either of you on taste or elegance, I have my own ideas of style and find them much in accordance with those of my future husband. Fitzwilliam will take me to town next Monday with Jane and Mary. We shall enlist Aunt Gardiner's help to pick all the necessary items. If that does not suit your desires, I shall wear the gown I wore to the Netherfield ball. It was good enough for Fitzwilliam to fall in love with me, so I think it will be good enough to secure him," Elizabeth said.

"But you do not know the best warehouses! You will not make a dress sufficient—"

Mrs Bennet's protests were interrupted by Lady Catherine. "You are joining the first circles, Elizabeth, and your dress must—"

"Enough!" Darcy said sharply, thoroughly startling both women into silence. He calmed himself before continuing. "Ladies, allow me to add my thanks for all you are doing on our behalf, but I can assure both of you that I know the Gardiners well. I trust that selecting Elizabeth's trousseau will not offer a challenge.

"I would beg you both to keep in mind that much of what drew me to admire Elizabeth had been influenced more by the Gardiners than by the Bennets." Darcy gave Mrs Bennet a contrite look. "I mean no offence, madam."

Much to Elizabeth's surprise, in less than five minutes, Lady Catherine and Mrs Bennet agreed that Darcy and Elizabeth were exceedingly odd people, and they had come together using unorthodox methods. If the Gardiners were responsible for it, who was to argue with success?

Elizabeth was delighted when the trip to town the following week went just as expected. The shopping occupied a mere three days and included fittings as well as trips to the opera and theatre. Why the colonel was required to escort Jane was not her business, or anybody else's, for that matter. The return to Longbourn was spent in merry enjoyment in the same coach Elizabeth had declined less than two months earlier.

The rest of the engagement period held several additional surprises.

Lydia had been denied a trip to Brighton, both for the wedding and because Darcy and the colonel bludgeoned Mr Bennet into submission. He had been prepared to allow Lydia a chance to 'learn her own insignificance at little trouble or expense'. That sentiment was enough to make the colonel lose his vaunted temper for the first time in Elizabeth's experience —and, she hoped, the last.

Colonel Fitzwilliam, along with Darcy, took all the young ladies, including Anne and Georgiana, for a tour of the camp followers' accommodations that had been set up outside of town. There, the colonel introduced them to some of the less fortunate military wives and asked them to describe their lives. That was enough to direct the minds of the younger Bennet girls away from the pursuit of soldiers—far away.

The trip also introduced Mary to Colonel Alton. The colonel had lost his left leg below the knee, so he would obviously never see battle again, but he had a secure position training troops and a small bit of money saved.

He was older than Mary, but not alarmingly so, and seemed smitten with her at first glance. The colonel called on her the next day, received a positive response, and the last few weeks of Darcy and Elizabeth's engagement found Mary and Colonel Alton reach an understanding. Both were extremely reticent, as well as respectful of Darcy and Elizabeth's engagement. There was no hurry, but the idea of an autumn wedding was generally found to be agreeable.

Another surprising alliance was forged between Lydia and Georgiana. They shared a common affliction in having been fooled by a scoundrel, and unexpectedly, that was enough of a connexion to surmount their entirely opposite personalities.

They spent enough time together that Darcy opined their differences in temperament would each even out and improve the other. When he decided to leave Georgiana behind at Longbourn for a month or three after the wedding, Colonel Fitzwilliam agreed. His only condition was that Lydia and Kitty had to take lessons with Georgiana, for which Elizabeth thought him a very sly fox indeed.

While Lydia and Georgiana grew their friendship over their shared differences, Anne and Kitty formed a bond over their mutual similarity. Elizabeth spent some time trying to work out why, but in the end, decided it did not matter. After all, she reasoned, if two ghosts standing in front of each other made them more noticeable, who was she to quibble?

Kitty spent nearly all her time at Netherfield with Anne when they were not attending shared entertainments. Neither lady could boast any of the traditional accomplishments. They sang badly and had long proved themselves inept with screens, paintbrushes, and pianofortes. Kitty could sew and trim bonnets well enough, so she taught Anne the skill. Anne had read enormously more, so she took on Kitty's belated education.

While their sisters forged friendships, Darcy and Elizabeth found joy walking and driving the paths around Hertfordshire, and somewhat belatedly, beginning riding lessons for Elizabeth. She had always preferred walking, but Darcy convinced her she could not truly view her own wilderness, let alone the peaks of Derbyshire, without riding. Reminding her that he would frequently be out on the grounds of Pemberley in places only accessible by riding, and most likely somewhat lonely, proved invaluable motivation.

The happy couple had the support of what was generally regarded as the two worst chaperons in Christendom. The colonel maintained that he had the eyes of a hawk and could spot a mouse from two hundred yards, but his boasts did not survive scrutiny. On the day he arrived with Jane at the top of Oakham Mount at the same time their charges arrived at Netherfield to escort Kitty back to Longbourn, even they had to admit they were not as diligent in their duties as expected.

Over the month, much to no one's surprise, the voluble, charming, short-tempered, and wary soldier fell quite in love with the quiet, composed but strong-willed lady who trusted everybody. His sentiments appeared to be reciprocated but no proposal was forthcoming.

Bingley repaid every debt of civility and attained credits with the neighbourhood. His lessons on estate management took hold, and Darcy found him not only diligent but legible in his work—a marked improvement.

More importantly, he had let go of any regard for Jane as she had for him. They might not be the most indifferent acquaintances in the world, but they could easily pass as such. Netherfield had been placed at the party's disposal, much to Kitty and Anne's delight.

One evening, a week before the wedding, Darcy asked Elizabeth, Jane, and Colonel Fitzwilliam to join him in the study at Netherfield. When they were all settled, Darcy turned to his cousin.

"I have what I expect will be our last problem with Wickham, and I hope you can assist me." He threw a small stack of papers on the table.

The colonel said nothing but looked at him curiously.

Darcy continued. "I paid the last of Wickham's debts to keep him out of gaol long enough to get killed in the navy. As part of that, I made him surrender all his assets. It seems he was in possession of an estate he won in a card game."

"If he owned an estate, why was he skulking around Meryton in a militia uniform?"

"Take a look."

The colonel inspected the first sheet, a report from Darcy's man of business. While it looked much like those he and Darcy examined as part of their duties for Rosings, it took a moment for the essentials to fall into place. He gave a soft whistle.

"This may be the worst estate in England."

Darcy laughed. "Overstating the case but it is close."

"Can you explain it for us?" asked Jane.

"Briarwood is about the size of Longbourn," the colonel replied. "It should have an annual income of two or three thousand pounds, but currently, it barely pays enough for the steward's salary. He seems to be managing but not for long. It is one flood away from reverting to the Crown."

Elizabeth looked at Darcy. "Why is that?"

"Decades of mismanagement, I would guess. Two-thirds of the fields seem to be abandoned. Half of the tenant cottages are damaged. The manor house is well constructed, but it is presently the domain of rats."

Both ladies shuddered, while the colonel turned to glare at Darcy.

"No!" he said.

"You do not even—"

"Whatever it is, no!"

Jane looked at Colonel Fitzwilliam. "Would it be too much trouble to understand what you are declining so vigorously?"

With his cousin too angry to speak, Darcy replied. "He believes I am about to take the best time-honoured approach to solving a problem."

"Which is?"

"Make it someone else's."

"Why not just give Briarwood away, sell it, or ignore it?" asked Elizabeth.

The colonel grumbled, "It is the blasted Darcy pride and honour—both of which are overdeveloped, in my humble opinion."

Both ladies looked to Darcy quizzically.

With a sigh, Darcy began. "Because it is my *obligation*. The owner of land has a duty to it and to those who make their living from it. It makes no difference how possession occurred. Once you own land, you own the obligation that goes with it, be it Pemberley or Briarwood.

"The local village, the tenants who remained there, the people who make their living from the estate—all are now under my protection. To be honest, I do not want it, and there are also legal issues."

"What could those be?" Elizabeth asked.

The colonel continued. "Certain things happen on estates that can end in local disputes or even the courts. Suppose a field floods, and it blocks a stream that goes to another estate, causing that estate to flood or the owner's herds to be depleted or die. The other estate owner can assess damages. It is an expensive proposition, only worthwhile if your opponent has deep pockets to go after."

"So, owning Briarwood is a detriment for the master of Pemberley?" Elizabeth asked.

"Absolutely," Darcy said. "The place has been gambled away and neglected for years. Nobody with any sense would have taken it since its value is actually negative."

Darcy gave Elizabeth a thoughtful look. "I would have to pay someone to take it in its present condition. If I gave it away, someone could restore it over a decade or two. It would grow quite valuable, but they would need some investment to do it."

Elizabeth smiled as comprehension dawned. "What if it were owned by a single individual with no other income—say, a retired colonel?"

"Then it would be safe, presuming he lived there and exerted reasonable control over the lands. In this hypothetical retired colonel's example, he would just fix the stream or negotiate a solution to the problem with the neighbour."

Jane looked between Darcy and the colonel. "You said, *if* he lived there?"

Darcy shrugged, "That would be best, but he could also just manage with a steward like most of his contemporaries. It is the management that is key, not the physical presence, although it would admittedly require a lot of that as well."

The colonel crossed his arms and grumbled. "I will not take charity."

Darcy began to form another argument when Jane cried, "*I will!*"

"Excuse me?" the colonel replied.

"I am not stupid," Jane said in a determined voice. "Lady Catherine runs Rosings with a little assistance from her nephews, so a woman can do it. I have a very clever sister, an educated father, an astute uncle, and the latest in a long line of prosperous landowners as my future brother. I am not afraid of hard work, and to be honest, life as a lady of leisure has left me perilously close to being the 'most beautiful' spinster in Meryton. I suspect an estate, even a terrible one, as my dowry would attract somebody."

Jane's studied avoidance of mentioning the colonel prompted a smile from her sister.

Darcy rubbed his chin in thought. "You know when you marry, it will become your husband's property unless we tie it up in a jointure or an entail, which would make it difficult to manage."

Jane smiled coyly. "Any man stupid enough to take on an estate like that deserves what he gets."

Elizabeth and Darcy burst out laughing, while the colonel only scowled, or at least, he tried to.

"For you, Jane, I would happily invest five thousand pounds. I had planned to supplement my new sisters' dowries, so yours would become your working capital," Darcy said.

At the look of disbelief on the faces of his intended and her sister, he said quickly, "My mother always wished for a half-dozen daughters, and my father planned his finances accordingly. I believe Lady Catherine might loan you another five thousand. If you married this lunkhead beside you, his father would put in another five at least—maybe ten. That would be enough to get Briarwood back up to scratch. It would take half a decade, but I would be happy to help you. The estate is but thirty miles from Pemberley, which Elizabeth would find convenient."

"We will do it!" Jane said.

The colonel, who had just taken a sip of tea, began choking.

"Do not make assumptions," Jane said drily as she patted his back. "If you wish to be part of that 'we', it requires but a single question. If not, there are others who will. I do not plan to undertake this endeavour alone, but make no mistake, I will be mistress of that estate."

Elizabeth, her eyes poring over the report, said impishly, "This manor house is terrible, Richard. It seems to be only twice as comfortable as a barracks."

He grumbled. "How long until someone points out the obvious benefit of not getting shot or bayonetted?"

"A battle easily won," Darcy said, chuckling. "You have gone soft. It appears the military may profit from your retirement."

The colonel took a deep breath, thought a moment, glared at his cousin and the man's intended, and said, "You two—go away!"

Darcy rose, offered his hand to Elizabeth, and led her, giggling, from the study. Resisting the temptation to loiter in the corridor, they had scarcely reached the drawing room when the happy couple caught up to announce their engagement.

With only a week to go, it would appear to some entirely impossible for both couples to share a wedding day, but with the swift thinking and actions of two gentlemen as well-connected as the grooms, it was not.

Epilogue

HAPPY FOR ALL HER MATERNAL FEELINGS WAS THE DAY ON which Mrs Bennet got rid of her two most deserving daughters. With what delighted pride she afterwards visited Mrs Fitzwilliam, and talked of Mrs Darcy, may only be guessed.

Well, strictly speaking, with both daughters living three days away in the wilds of Derbyshire—and Mrs Fitzwilliam living in what Mrs Bennet was quite certain was a draughty old castle—and herself entirely too occupied with Lady Catherine, Mrs Bennet never actually visited either of them. Her daughters and their husbands came to visit Longbourn regularly, so what was the point of undertaking a long carriage ride?

Jane did not in fact live in a draughty old castle. Briarwood became first a prosperous estate, and with the gradual change from agriculture to industry, eventually became a hub of a railroad, and then a burgeoning industrial centre. Pemberley did the same, although since its agriculture was much better established, it was a decade or so behind Briarwood.

Mr Bingley never left Netherfield, and in fact, purchased it a year after the double wedding of the century. He became a man of quiet competence and industry and was always on the closest terms with the Fitzwilliams and Darcys even before he finally, after three years of effort, managed to convince Anne to surrender the de Bourgh name in favour of Bingley.

Anne had discovered that she was not quite as sanguine with a short life of indolence and entertainment as she had once thought. One day, a few months before her dear friend Kitty's wedding to John Lucas, the bride-to-be asked Anne her opinion of Mr Bingley and was surprised by the answer.

"He is just what a young man ought to be," said she, "sensible, good-humoured, lively—and I never saw such happy manners!"

They burst into laughter, perfectly aware she sounded like Jane before she went through her brief heartbreak, now only vaguely remembered, over the self-same gentleman.

"Mr Bingley looks at you a great deal," Kitty said.

Anne scoffed. "He used to look at Jane a great deal, too."

Not to be dissuaded, Kitty said, "You were not there. I was. He looks at you differently."

"How so?"

Kitty shrugged. "He looked at Jane the way a boy looks at a girl. He looks at you like a man looks at a woman."

Anne could only manage a squeak. "Oh my! What should I do?"

"I cannot answer that, aside from the advice I think one of my sisters once gave the other, but I cannot remember which."

"Go on."

"Decide how you will answer if he asks for something," advised Kitty. "He may ask outright, or simply start treating you in a way that you could interpret as a suggestion of further intimacy. If you have your answer worked out in advance, you are not forced to think of one without time for contemplation. Lizzy assures me that can go very badly."

"Did it go badly for her? I cannot see that it did."

"No, but it could have. A chance comment made by the colonel set in motion a chain of events that turned out well and disrupted another story that would have gone very badly. Lizzy was unwilling to explain it to me at the time, but I suspect she would be happy to talk to you."

"Yes, I should say she is relatively secure in her position and her husband's affections now."

Both ladies laughed, but it did put the thought in Anne's mind, and half a year later, Catherine Lucas stood up with her good friend as she became Mrs Charles Bingley.

Much like the Fitzwilliams of Briarwood, the Bingleys entered the new age well-prepared. Bingley found an able assistant in his mother-in-law, who lived with them at Netherfield until the end of her life, after she gave up the yoke of Rosings back to the de Bourgh family.

Lady Catherine found that removing the weight of responsibility from her shoulders thoroughly changed her disposition. She remained good friends with Mrs Bennet, who moved to Netherfield upon Mr Bennet's death some years later, even though Mrs Collins insisted she was welcome at Longbourn. Mrs Bennet declared that one mistress was entirely enough for one estate but was hard-pressed to explain why Netherfield needed three.

To the surprise of no one or everyone, depending on when the person formed their immutable first impressions, Lydia Bennet and Georgiana Darcy became the belles of the ball in their first Season. They attracted any number of suitors, as befitted two such lively but well-mannered ladies.

Much to Darcy and Elizabeth's joy, their sisters' personalities evened out to produce two young ladies who combined the best features of manners, grace, fashion, and surprisingly, an iron-cored adherence to propriety.

During their second Season, each found a gentleman who suited them. Both Georgiana and Lydia were under the protection of Fitzwilliam Darcy at the time. Marriage and fatherhood had mellowed him considerably in the intervening years, so their suitors were allowed to pursue them with only minimal teasing.

Seasons passed. Life went on. Children and grandchildren were born. In due time, the Bennet sisters and their husbands were laid to rest in their family crypts. Their memories were kept in sharp relief by their children, in fuzzy remembrance by their grandchildren, and in a general sense of gratitude by their great-grandchildren.

In time, as the world changed around them, and they changed with it, none of those various descendants would ever be aware that their entire lives pivoted around a single sentence voiced in Kent sometime in the year 1812. All they knew was that their parents encouraged them to follow the family tradition of keeping first impressions under good regulation and striving with all their might to gather the information necessary to reach the point where they could correctly say, "That explains everything."

ACKNOWLEDGMENTS

I would like to acknowledge all the help and feedback from my online readers. The community has always been welcoming, supportive and instrumental in honing my craft.

Special thanks to Joy King (J Dawn King), who read my second story and very kindly wrote telling me I had 'the makings'. She taught me some of the cardinal rules of JAFF and was a big help when I was starting out.

I've also had lots of helpful discussions with other writers who gave me tips, critiques, ideas, and encouragement. Particular thanks to Gianna Thomas, Anne Morris, Elizabeth Frerichs, Casandra B Leigh, Nicky Roth, prhood, Babsy1221, leavesfallingup, and sysa22.

I'd especially like a shout-out to my Quills & Quartos team who helped refine and polish the story for your reading pleasure: Jan Ashton, Amy D'Orazio and Debbie Styne.

ABOUT THE AUTHOR

Wade H. Mann is the pen name for Wade Hatler. Wade is a retired software geek, living near Seattle with his lovely wife Amalia, who he met in Spain, halfway through a 12,000-mile, 18-country, recumbent bike trip.

He has been writing JAFF since 2017, and has produced 1.4 million words about Darcy, Elizabeth, and the whole P&P family.

Wade spent 30 years making software to improve the lives of cancer patients. His software is currently used to treat two million patients per year all over the world. The capstone of his career was building an independent medical-software company that was successfully acquired.

He grew up in a sawmill, so he can probably claim the mantle of the only lumberjack-geek-romance writer around.

Wade posts as WadeH on the fan fiction boards. His travel writings can be found at www.wademan.com.

g

FROM THE PUBLISHER

The favour of your rating or review would be greatly appreciated.

Subscribers to the Quills & Quartos mailing list receive advance notice of sales, bonus content, and giveaways. You can join our mailing list at www.QuillsandQuartos.com where you will also find excerpts from recent releases.